Spirits Between Series

Volume IX

Phantom
in
the **Bedchamber**

Ed Okonowicz

Spirits Between the Bays
Volume IX
Phantom in the Bedchamber
First Edition

ISBN 1-890690-05-8

Published by
Myst and Lace Publishers, Inc.
1386 Fair Hill Lane
Elkton, Maryland 21921

Printed in the U.S.A.
by Victor Graphics

Cover Art, Typography and Design
by Kathleen Okonowicz

Dedications

In memory of Bob Cohen,
an excellent photographer and a special friend.
He will be missed, but remembered so very fondly.
Ed Okonowicz

To Larry and Helen Burgoon, my aunt and uncle.
You are a special part of my childhood memories.
Kathleen Burgoon Okonowicz

Acknowledgments

The author and illustrator appreciate the assistance of those
who have played an important role in this project.
Special thanks are extended to
George Steitz, Bill and Amber Madl and William Staker
for their valuable assistance;
and to

Barbara Burgoon
Sue Moncure
Marianna Dyal
Ted Stegura and
Monica Witkowski
for their proofreading and suggestions;

and, of course,

particular appreciation to the ghosts and their hosts.

Also available from Myst and Lace Publishers, Inc.

Spirits Between the Bays Series

Volume I
Pulling Back the Curtain
(October, 1994)

Volume II
Opening the Door
(March, 1995)

Volume III
Welcome Inn
(September, 1995)

Volume IV
In the Vestibule
(August, 1996)

Volume V
Presence in the Parlor
(April, 1997)

Volume VI
Crying in the Kitchen
(April, 1998)

Volume VII
Up the Back Stairway
(April, 1999)

Volume VIII
Horror in the Hallway
(September, 1999)

Volume IX
Phantom in the Bedchamber
(June, 2000)

DelMarVa Murder Mystery Series
FIRED!
(May, 1998)

Halloween House
(May, 1999)

Stairway over the Brandywine
A Love Story
(February, 1995)

Possessed Possessions
Haunted Antiques, Furniture and Collectibles
(March, 1996)

Possessed Possessions 2
More Haunted Antiques, Furniture and Collectibles
(September, 1998)

Disappearing Delmarva
Portraits of the Peninsula People
(August, 1997)

Table of Contents

Site is open to the public.

  Story is about a haunted possession.

Introduction

C ivil War ghosts and lighthouse spirits are featured in *Phantom in the Bed Chamber*, Vol. IX of our *Spirits Between the Bays* ghost/folklore series.

From Gettysburg's Farnsworth House Inn Bed and Breakfast to Point Lookout State Park in Maryland, site of the "nation's largest Civil War prison," spirited activity abounds. Interestingly, Point Lookout also is home to what some people consider the "most haunted lighthouse in America," and that 1830 historic beacon also is featured in this volume.

For those who want to shop in a haunted store, downtown Dover's Delaware Made shop is worth a visit. And what better place to take the kids on a summer afternoon for a scoop of ice cream than to New Castle's Cellar Gourmet, which has a ghost named Jane roaming its haunted basement eatery.

This volume also provides a behind-the-scene look at a group of New Jersey ghost hunters, an interview with a mother and daughter who live in a hexed Eastern Shore plantation house, a report from two Delmarva residents who spent vacations in a haunted Florida beach home, an eerie visit from a deceased doll collector in Annapolis, the appearance of a phantom dog lover in Grantsville, Maryland, and a first-hand report on what it's like to transport a dead body.

In our Short Sightings section, you will read about the "Unquiet Grave" in St. Augustine, Maryland, a duplicate New

England home that hexed its builders, more eerie tales from Fort Delaware, a mysterious force that helped find a missing set of rings and a ghost that apparently has followed a family into its new home in the First State.

Readers interested in visiting haunted sites will find eight public locations featured in this book, and each is marked with a bat symbol. Regarding accessible public haunted locations, this book is second only to *Welcome Inn*, Vol. III, which features 12 haunted inns, restaurants and museums. Next in this ghost-sites-to-visit category is Vol. VI, *Crying in the Kitchen*, which offers six spirited sites that are open to the public.

We appreciate your patronage and enjoy meeting many of you at public events and book signings. We hope you'll enjoy these stories, and our series will continue with Vol. X, *Seance in the Study*.

Happy Hauntings.

—Ed Okonowicz
in Fair Hill, Maryland,
at the northern edge
of the Delmarva Peninsula
—Summer 2000

the
HISTORIC
FARNSWORTH
HOUSE INN

Farnsworth House Inn and Restaurant

No trip to Gettysburg, Pennsylvania, is complete without a stop at the Farnsworth House, a stately, pre-Civil War-era building housing a restaurant, inn and assorted shops, located in the center of the town's historic district. Standing proudly along the edge of Baltimore Street, this brick, three-story structure is one of a handful of survivors of Gettysburg's fine inns and taverns. Over the last century and a half, progress has devoured much of the town's architectural history related to inns, taverns, shops and small family businesses. At the beginning of the 21st century, this fascinating remnant provides visitors and locals a glimpse of the places where travelers rested and dined while passing through the area nearly two centuries ago.

The Farnsworth, as it is called, also played a role in the great Civil War battle that took place in, around and through the small Pennsylvania town in July 1863. When tourists pay a visit to the sites of the great battles and small skirmishes that occurred at this Civil War crossroads, many choose to stay or dine at the Farnsworth House. Over the last 25 years, it has become one of the "must" sites to see.

3

But before we delve too deeply into the building's historical significance and its modern day attractions, it's important to state that the Farnsworth House is especially known for its ghosts. While this "Showplace of the Civil War," as the home is sometimes described, has seen its share of visitors (both famous and non), its owners, staff and guests also speak of unusual sounds and sights. These unexplained events occur so often, that many believe—very firmly, and speak very openly—that the Farnsworth House has an ample stable of entities—be they apparitions, phantoms or unearthly visitors—from another time or dimension. These spirits seem to have taken up residence within the structure's dated walls and appear to have thrived amidst the antiques, period furnishings and artwork. Most importantly, they apparently are not shy about making their presence known.

First Impressions

My first visit to the Farnsworth House was on a March weekend in 1999 when I was speaking at the annual Gettysburg Ghost Conference. Almost immediately upon my arrival, conference guests and other speakers advised me to "visit the Farnsworth," which I did. After taking a quick tour, I promised to return to conduct a more thorough investigation and interview.

In August, five months later, my wife, Kathleen, and I arrived in Gettysburg. After receiving a tour of the Farnsworth House complex, we took seats in the tavern and spent several hours speaking with Bev Bittle, a long-time area resident, who for the last eight years has been an employee of the Farnsworth House.

At a polished wooden table, and surrounded by antiques and walls lined with Civil War memorabilia and photographs, Bev shared hundreds of details about the Farnsworth House's history, visitors, staff and, of course, its ghosts. It was during the tour and this conversation that I learned that the Farnsworth is more than a hotel and restaurant. It also includes a group of adjacent shops specializing in fine artwork, military relics and books on the Civil War and related topics. For those interested in the macabre, there are the Farnsworth House Candlelight Ghost Walks along the town's streets and dramatic ghost story presentations in the underground Mourning Theatre.

For anyone planning a trip to Gettysburg, the Farnsworth should be, at the very least, a place to visit, for it is a destination to savor rather than a quick stop along the way to the monument accented battlefield. It is a location where one can appreciate the atmosphere of a time that has long since faded away.

The History

The Farnsworth House is dedicated to perpetuating the memory of the brave soldiers who fought on both sides during the Civil War.

The original section of the house was built in 1810. The adjoining brick structure that faces Baltimore Street was added by John McFarland in 1833. The Sweney family occupied the house during the 1863 battle. Eventually, the dwelling was opened as a lodging site by the George E. Black family in the early 1900s. Original flooring, walls and rafters remain intact, a tribute to the excellent quality of work by early craftsmen.

During the battle, the house sheltered Confederate sharpshooters, one of whom is believed to have accidentally shot Jennie Wade, who is the only civilian known to have died in the three-day battle. The south side of the house gives an indication of the fierceness of the fighting that raged throughout the town. More than 100 bullet holes can still be seen, scattered throughout the three-story-tall brick wall.

The house was named in memory of Elon John Farnsworth. On the eve of the battle, he was promoted to the rank of brigadier general. Soon after the failure of Pickett's charge against the Union forces on July 3, Farnsworth's regiments were ordered to charge against the right flank of Longstreet's position. In this ill fated charge, Farnsworth and 65 of his men perished.

In 1972, the building was purchased by its present owners, the Loring H. Shultz family, and work began immediately to restore the Farnsworth House to its 1863 appearance.

The owners have stated that their goal is to, "provide our guests an experience reminiscent of the Civil War era."

House tours for groups can be arranged by appointment. These are conducted by guides in period dress and visitors hear of the dramatic experiences of Gettysburg civilians during the battle. The tour begins in the old cellar. Many stories are related to the Union Army retreat through the streets immediately around the Farnsworth House, and most of the townspeople spent several days hiding in their own basements to avoid the fighting and danger that was raging throughout the town. A highlight of the escorted expedition is a visit to the inn's low-beamed attic, where Confederate sharpshooters hid and shot at Union forces.

A grand reproduction of an historic photograph, taken Nov. 19, 1863, which consumes a large portion of a wall near the bar in the tavern, shows the procession of President Abraham Lincoln on Baltimore Street en route to the cemetery where he delivered the Gettysburg Address. The Farnsworth House can be seen in this impressive antique photograph.

Also worth noting is the 30-foot-long and 6-foot-high glass case along an entire wall in the Farnsworth bar, which is known as the "Killer Angels Tavern." It is named in honor of the book by author Michael Shaara, who wrote the novel that later became the basis for the movie *Gettysburg*. Behind the glass case is a display of items used during the filming of the movie. The large number of the film's actors and production crew became "regulars" at the Farnsworth House tavern, and their clothing, uniforms, weapons and autographs are on display.

As Bev Bittle, our hostess told us in August, "All the actors drank here during the filming. They would come in at night, and it was a wild and crazy time. The people who frequent this bar as regulars are authors, historians, sculptors, park guides and rangers. This is a Civil War hangout. We never have baseball games on the television. We have the History Channel. Any guest who stays with us quickly realizes that this is a cultural center for conversation. They're not interested in who won the Phillies' game. They talk about maneuvers during the battle, flanking fire, why certain generals made the decisions they did and what might

6

have happened if things were done differently. It's fascinating to sit back and listen. There are so many aspects of what goes on here that create a gravitational pull of intellectual people and Civil War buffs and history buffs, which is great."

Bev paused and reflected on the area of Gettysburg itself, a region that she described as being unlike any other because of the battle and because the area has become a living shrine to the men who had died there.

"Working here is hard to describe," Bev said. "You are totally steeped in history at all times. I sincerely don't believe you can live and work in a town like Gettysburg without being fully aware of appreciating what happened here 135 years ago," she added, pausing. "Everything we do perpetuates what occurred."

The Haunts

When I asked Bev how many ghost stories or unusual events she has heard about the Farnsworth House over the years, she paused only a brief second to take time to smile, and replied casually, "We've had hundreds of reports, literally hundreds. It is not unusual to us. I check people in and out of the inn five to seven days a week, and I hear two to three new reports each week. Many people come here well aware of our reputation, and they are aware of the rooms with activity."

Bev recited a list of the usual types of unusual things her guests and coworkers have reported. They include:
- Walking in the halls,
- Strange footsteps,
- The sound of things being dragged in the attic,
- Cold drafts,
- Moaning and
- Sightings.

"The reports come from every room, even in the back section of the house," she said.

But some rooms are believed to have more activity than others. The Sara Black Room and the Catherine Sweney Room both have been reported as the most active sites by workers and guests.

The Sara Black Room is named after a previous owner of the building. Bev said it is considered to be the most haunted room in the establishment. There have been reports of moaning, dragging across the floor, footsteps in the hallway and apparitions.

7

"One guest said she saw someone sitting on the bed," Bev recalled. "And she even reported seeing a depression in the mattress. Also, some people have seen movement of the wedding gown that is displayed on a mannequin. One woman said she actually saw an arm of the gown raise up in the air."

Two months after I visited the Farnsworth House, I met a lady during a program I was giving at the Chesapeake Bay Maritime Museum. She recalled that she and her husband had spent an overnight in the Sara Black Room. The afternoon they arrived, she said she had purchased her husband a new shirt. They removed it from the packaging and hung it in the closet to help remove the wrinkles.

When they awoke the next morning, her husband opened the closet door to grab his shirt, and he noticed that all of the buttons were missing. They found them scattered on the closet floor. It was as if someone had taken a razor blade and cut them off the brand new shirt.

Bev said more than one guest has reported hearing the sound of a jew's harp performing music of the Civil War period. The instrument is not being played loudly, and it's said that the sound seems to be coming from the front area of the Bed and Breakfast section of the inn.

"We get frequent requests for the 'haunted room,' " Bev said. "Some of these rooms are booked six months in advance for Halloween. I got one call and the man said, 'The moon will be full on Saturday night. I want the Sara Black Room.' We don't just get repeat customers," she said, smiling, "we get, repeat, repeat, repeat customers."

Guests watching the programs in The Mourning Theatre in the building's cellar have reported seeing the figure of a Confederate soldier in the background, behind the storyteller.

"In the last year," Bev said, "that has occurred about four times. That really stops the show."

There also are sighting of the apparition they call "Mary," who is believed to be the spirit of a previous owner. What's interesting about this ghost, Bev said, is that she's seen more often than the soldier and she is more "clearly defined," not a misty type sighting. She has been reported in the first-floor dining room by visitors and servers. On other occasions, she has been sighted behind the bar, taking inventory of the stock. "But," Bev said, "she is so real, that some people think it is a reenactor in costume who has lost her way."

It was during a weekend in the middle of March 2000, when I was speaking at the annual Gettysburg Ghost Conference, that I returned to the Farnsworth House. This time, my wife, Kathleen, and I stayed in the Sara Black Room. Upon checking in, we met Donna Withrow, who had been working at the Farnsworth for a little over a year. When she showed us into our room, I asked her about the resident ghosts. She smiled, then replied that she certainly had heard all of the stories, and she also had a few tales of her own that she was willing to share.

On Saturday evening, Kathleen and I enjoyed Donna's wonderful storytelling performance in The Mourning Theatre.

With a black coffin and flickering candles as a backdrop, Donna told ghost stories set both in and near Gettysburg that caused the appreciative audience members' blood to chill quite frequently.

After that formal session, sitting in the spooky sub-level room that had seen its share of phantom visitors, the performer dressed in Victorian garb, spoke in hushed tones. It was as if Donna was afraid to be overheard by unseen eavesdroppers as she shared her versions of the ghosts in the Farnsworth.

"A psychic came here," Donna recalled, "and she said that we have 14 spirits, and seven of them are identified. In fact, two visit the theatre quite often."

She said the primary regular patron is a little seven-year-old boy, who was trampled to death by a horse. Apparently, Donna explained, young boys in the early 1900s used to amuse themselves by hiding in the narrow street on the side of the Farnsworth House. As a game, they would take turns jumping out in front of horsedrawn carriages riding along Baltimore Street. The boy who came the closest to the horses that he surprised was the winner.

Unfortunately, in winning the game, one young child lost big time—his life. On a sunny day in the early 1900s, the boy jumped out in front of a buggy and was run down and stomped upon by the terrified horse. Neighbors rushed the injured child into the Farnsworth House, but nothing could be done. It's believed that he died in the Sara Black Room.

Sometimes, Donna said, visitors see a crying spirit of the boy's father walking the halls, carrying the small child who is wrapped in a gray blanket. Also, employees believe the child ghost enjoys playing with the indoor plumbing—since the toilets

9

flush on their own—and he likes to turn the radio on and change the stations.

Mary, Donna said, is the premier ghost of the inn, and she resides most often in the Sara Black Room. Legend is that Mary was a midwife. While delivering a baby in that particular room, the newborn child died. People believe that Mary cannot cope with the fact that she lost the baby, and Mary's troubled spirit roams the house trying to care for anyone who needs attention.

The ghost's presence can be detected by an overpowering scent of flowers, the swishing sound of a skirt in the hallway and by a sudden feeling of coldness. Mary also has been known to tap guests on the shoulder and move things around in the Sara Black Room and its bathroom.

On several occasions, guests have seen the mattress in the Sara Black Room depress. It sometimes occurs while guests are sleeping in the bed. Donna said that inn workers tell the guests not to be alarmed—it's just Mary taking a little nap. Mary, too, sometimes catches performances in The Mourning Theatre. Her ghost has been seen in the rear of the room at the foot of the stairs that lead into the first floor of the inn.

Donna said her most disturbing experience while performing in the cellar theatre took place the night that a distinct black shadow literally flew down the main aisle while she was speaking.

The storyteller said the black shadow incident was her most bothersome paranormal experience since working in the inn. All of the other apparitions and ghostly manifestations—whether through smell, sound or temperature change—have been easy to deal with.

"I've never been really afraid," Donna said. "Besides, I believe Mary is here and she protects us."

In 1863, the attic of the house—also called the garret—is where Confederate sharpshooters fired at Yankee troops during the battle in the midst of town. A few years ago, the garret was used as an inn guest room. There is a story, Donna said, about a young boy, who was staying in the top level room with his mother. One night, he got up in the middle of the night to use the second-floor bathroom, since there is no toilet facility in the garret. When the boy turned on the second-floor bathroom light, he began screaming, claiming that blood was all over the walls. When other guests who had been awakened by his screams arrived, they saw nothing like what the boy described.

But, Donna said, over the years other guests have reported seeing blood on the walls.

While performing in The Mourning Theatre, Donna said she has seen the little boy ghost, sitting in the rear row in a chair along the aisle. In fact, at the beginning of each of her storytelling performances, she advises patrons to "leave the chair in the back open for the little boy, who may be stopping by tonight."

In the Farnsworth House Bookstore, Donna pulled out a few sheets of paper from behind the counter and passed them to us. They were submitted by guests who had experienced ghostly or unexplained incidents. When asked how many reports the inn has collected over the years, Donna said there are boxes filled with similar testimonials.

On the Air

It was on the Thursday evening before Halloween in 1999 when members of Rouse and Company, broadcast over WQSR-FM—Baltimore's award winning oldies station—stayed overnight in the Farnsworth House.

"We called around," said Steve Rouse, leader of the zany morning drive-time program, "and were told by a number of sources that Gettysburg was the most haunted place in America."

Eventually, they ended up staying in the Farnsworth House, one of the most haunted inns in America.

Steve said the WQSR staff had the run of the inn, sleeping in a number of haunted rooms. They said they were up most of the night, listening for footsteps, creaking doors and voices and hoping to see a few apparitions. According to Maynard G and Steve, they weren't disappointed.

Maynard said they spent a fair amount of time in the garret. That's where they noticed that every time they securely shut the door to that small room, the moment they turned away and focused their attention elsewhere, the door would be open.

"We did everything we could to make it open when we were there," Maynard said, including checking the latch and jumping on the floor to cause vibrations. "At those times, it would stay closed. But when we turned away, the door would not remain shut."

He also mentioned an unusual incident associated with an antique, metal baby carriage that sits on the landing of the inn's second floor, very close to the stairs heading up to the garret. When they came down from the top floor, Maynard noticed that the carriage had been moved—it was facing in a different direction and two of its wheels were resting on the steps leading up to the garret. No living person was around who could have moved the object.

Steve said they broadcast from the Mourning Theatre on Friday morning. He recalled that late in the show, several members of the Baltimore Ghost Hunters group came running down into the cellar because their instrument indicated that the temperature had deviated dramatically in one of the rooms, dropping from around 50 degrees to well below zero.

"At one point while broadcasting," Steve said, "I recall the smell or stench of death. It was very distinct."

But he and the rest of the group agreed that it was in the "Catacombs"—a small tunnel-like, dirt-floored area only accessible through a side door of the Mourning Theatre—where the most frightening incident occurred.

Maynard, two ghost hunters and Vickie, a clairvoyant, were inside the narrow tunnel. Suddenly, Maynard recalled, "Vickie seemed to be bothered and said, 'We have to get out of here.' "

Without hesitation, everyone raced toward the exit door and Maynard said he felt something tugging on his pant leg. And when he exited from the catacombs, Maynard said he had a muddy handprint on his pant leg, which others verified that they saw. He added that he thought he also heard the sound of a crying child in the tunnel area.

Maynard said that he can't be positive if everything that happened during their stay was related to some paranormal force or activity. "Maybe part of it was us being ready to see something," he said. "But the ghosts or whatever they were didn't let us down."

Steve admitted he was skeptical before making the trip to Gettysburg. "I was like, 'Oh, yeah! Right!' But that trip sold me on the fact that there was something there. We went there for the fun of it, and thought it would be kind of interesting. But when the show was over everyone was in the basement, and I had to go in the inn and walk to my second floor room. I got the eeriest feeling as I headed up those stairs, realizing that I was there all by myself. I was glad to be out of there."

Slight Movements

According to Bev, all of the waitstaff and bartenders have had the feeling that there has been slight movement, or something has walked past them. There also are frequent reports of another lady dressed in black roaming the building.

Oftentimes, Bev said, guests will say nothing during their stay. But as they are checking out they will report, as casually as possible, "I don't believe in this, but, let me tell you what happened last night." Bev said she believes it's a "rationalizing process" that is designed to provide the speaker with some level of self protection.

"I don't even have to look for activity in the Farnsworth House," Bev said. "It comes to meet me head on."

Apparently, word of the Farnsworth ghosts has spread.

Arts & Entertainment Network did a film sequence on the inn's ghost stories in April 1999. Tales about unusual events at the house have been featured in the *Baltimore Sun* and *Philadelphia Inquirer*. The BBC visited in the summer of 1999, and a program with a segment on the Farnsworth House is planned to air on The Learning Channel in 2000.

In addition to the site being a magnet for ghost hunters, the inn's visitors have come from as far away as England, Germany and other foreign sites.

"We, literally, have an international clientele," Bev said. "We're the only restaurant in Gettysburg that has ever been featured in *Bon Appetit*."

Having grown up in the area around Gettysburg, Bev said she and her friends were always aware of the Farnsworth House and its historic and eerie reputation. "The Farnsworth House was haunted before it became fashionable to be haunted," she said.

Bev's first unusual experience in the house wasn't anything dramatic, more like an awareness that there was something there, looking over her shoulder.

"At different times all over the house," Bev said, "you will get the feeling that you have just missed seeing something as it moved. Your first reaction is, 'I really didn't see that.' Then you attempt, *ad infinitum*, to rationalize that it couldn't have been anything. But even though you accept that they're here, it's still so unexpected when it happens."

Some people make fun of ghosts or roll their eyes when they hear about unexplained events. That is not the case at the Farnsworth House. "We don't treat ghosts lightly," Bev said. "We can appreciate the spirits of the men who laid down their lives here."

Throughout our conversation, Bev provided lesser known facts about the town's past—mentioning how in 1863 Gettysburg was a sleepy little village of 2,400 people. Suddenly, it was overrun with tens of thousands of soldiers, and was right in the middle of a major battle that took place in its streets and countryside.

People lived in their cellars for days. Bullet holes pierced the walls of residences, outhouses and barns. War arrived suddenly and left death on the doorsteps of the residents.

In the attic of the Bed and Breakfast building, Confederate sharpshooters dragged trunks across the floor and used them for protection as they lay in the top floor window and shot at the Yankees in the streets below.

On certain nights, guests say they can hear the sound of an unseen phantom dragging a chest across the same floorboards that were walked on during the Civil War. Is it history repeated over and over by a ghost trapped in the past? Who can say for sure if it is, or it isn't?

More than a Bed and Breakfast

There are nine guest rooms, five in the main house and four in a more recent addition located off the garden and tavern. In the brick building, guests can stay in rooms named Sara Black, Catherine Sweney (the two most haunted), Jennie Wade, McFarland and Shultz. In the newer section are rooms named after Belle Boyd (Confederate spy), Custer, Lincoln and Eisenhower.

The main dining room is accented by oil paintings of the two opposing commanding officers at Gettysburg, Gen. Robert E. Lee and Gen. George G. Meade. Guests dine by candlelight among such artifacts as Civil War photographs by Matthew Brady, original artwork and sculptures.

Garden dining in season takes place in an open-air setting beside a spring-fed stream that was used by soldiers from both the Union and Confederate armies. A special pedestal features a bust of Gen. Farnsworth, created by Norman Annis, the same artist who sculpted the Eisenhower statue at Gettysburg College.

The *Killer Angels Tavern* offers beverages and food throughout the year. It's on-site Civil War "library," an extensive collection of books, maps and reference documents, is used often to resolve disputes among patrons who continue to analyze and re-fight the local battle. During reenactment weekends and celebrations in Gettysburg, soldiers in full dress uniforms can be found inside the tavern entertaining patrons and discussing the Civil War.

The *Art and Book Gallery* contains paintings and books associated with the Civil War. The gallery offers hundreds of prints and is an exclusive dealer for Don Troiani, America's most respected military artist, and Ron Tunison, America's most admired historical sculptor. The bookstore contains thousands of volumes.

Gettysburg Quartermaster, displays thousands of military items from the Revolutionary War to Vietnam, and specializing in the Civil War and World War II. These include swords, uniforms, bullets, tools, buttons, documents, accessories and military relics.

Aces High War Haus Gallery specializes in WWI and WWII limited edition prints, books and photographs signed by some of the world's greatest aviation heroes.

Summary

One cannot visit Gettysburg without becoming a captive of its history. Ghost hunters who think they will visit to capture orbs or spirit energy on film, or hear hair raising tales of the unexplained, cannot leave this town unaffected by the heroic events that took place in 1863.

In all of my ghost investigations over the years, I have learned that history and horror are interrelated. It is rare to find one without the other. There must be a source for each unearthly event, each bizarre disturbance. Oftentimes, the forgotten cause—a murder, suicide, sudden death, tragic accident or slow demise on a battlefield—is eventually discovered. At Gettysburg the source is apparent. It is often known before the quest begins.

Some say the town and farmland that hosted the most famous battle of the Civil War also is the most haunted site in America. That may well be. But one cannot truly appreciate the ghost stories that Gettysburg has provided without studying and understanding its historic significance. To ignore the tragedy and the heroic deeds of the brave men who were wounded and died here would do them and oneself a great injustice.

Attractions: Dining room, Victorian-era accommodations in nine guest rooms, outside garden dining in season, house tour and museum, ghost walks nightly, theatre ghost story performances, several associated stores with books, artwork, military artifacts.

The *Gettysburg* film props, on display in the tavern display case, include Chamberlain's hat, coat and boots (Jeff Daniels), Longstreet's shirt (Tom Berenger), Buford's shirt (Sam Elliott), Pickett's sash and frock coat (Stephen Lang), Lee's hat (Martin Sheen), and Armistead's gloves (Richard Jordon). Don't be surprised to see a video of *Gettysburg* running continuously on a television in the Killer Angels Tavern.

Sightings: Throughout the complex, particularly in the Sara Black Room and the Catherine Sweney Room, also in the Dining Room, Mourning Theatre and Killer Angels Tavern.

Contact: Farnsworth House, 401 Baltimore Street, Gettysburg, PA 17325; telephone: (717) 334-8838; web site: <www.gettysburg address.com>; e-mail: <farnhaus@mail.cvn.net>.

Haunted House
Near the Water

It's interesting how I find out about these haunted house stories. In this case, I was alerted by Les Pearson. He and his wife, Nancy, are owners of Pearson's Suburban Flag Headquarters, a wonderful shop in Stanton, Delaware, that features hundreds of First State items for sale, plus flags of all sizes and from every state and scores of countries. The couple has carried all of our books since we began releasing them in 1994, and their business was a sponsor of my *Ghost Talk* cable television show several years ago.

It was in December when I hit the button on my answering machine and heard Les announce, "Ed. You've got to give me a call right away. I've got a woman in here from over in Maryland. She just bought your whole set of ghost books and wants to tell you about her friend, who's got a place on the Eastern Shore. She says her friend has ghosts all over her house—in the cellar, upstairs. Several people have seen them. Get back to me as soon as you can."

Knowing Les, I figured I better respond quickly since he probably was keeping the customer captive in his shop waiting for me to return his call. Luckily, I got back to him in time. He had me speak to Harriett, who gave me the telephone number of the two owners of the haunted house—her best friend Marge, who lived in the old mansion with her 20-year-old daughter Susan.

17

About two weeks later, on New Year's Eve, I was headed south along the western side of Delmarva to meet with the two ladies at their haunted home. It was early in the afternoon, less than 12 hours before the arrival of the year 2000 and its much publicized Y2K bug, when I entered the old gray-siding farmhouse that stood atop a knoll overlooking a winding river that emptied into the upper Chesapeake Bay.

Marge and Susan were waiting for me. The older woman was a retiree and a faithful reader of the *Sprits* series. She knew all about the other people I had met over the years. She said she was eager to share her stories and hoped I would write up her experiences so other people fascinated with ghosts could learn about them. Her daughter Susan, who worked at a nearby retirement home, also was willing to talk about the unusual things she had seen and heard over the last two years. They explained that they noticed strange events as soon as they started restoring the old home.

Private Tour

Susan announced that the first item of business was giving me a house tour. But this was nothing like the annual spring garden club walk-throughs or those decorated Christmas candlelight excursions sponsored by small town ladies societies. There were no hosts clad in period costumes pointing out boring historic highlights, no experts droning on about the delicate feature of the furniture and no collection to help preserve the architectural treasures of this last-of-its-kind historic manse.

On the contrary, Marge and Susan led me through the first floor's restored living, dining and music rooms and country kitchen very quickly. Occasionally, they pointed proudly to some restoration work they had done themselves and their exciting discoveries—like the fireplace they found hidden behind a wall of cheap, warped paneling.

The next stop was the second floor, where I viewed the master and guest bedrooms and the office area where a modern computer sat in a room that had been built more than 250 years ago.

These restored areas were interesting, and the owners were proud of the results of their hard work. But, the more fascinating spots seemed to be the old building's out-of-the-way cubbyholes and secret crannies—places that were still on the list awaiting restoration. These sites included the dirt cellar, servants' quarters, "room to nowhere" and a small tunnel entrance (discovered under a trap door concealed in the kitchen closet).

About 15 minutes later, seated on old wooden chairs at an antique table in the dining room—with bright sun reflecting off the exposed wide-plank floor—the three of us talked about the house, its history and, of course, its sprits. I wanted to know why two women from North Wilmington had decided to sell their contemporary development home and move to the middle of nowhere and take on a major renovation project.

"I always wanted to live in an old, historic house," Susan said. "And my mother and I are the best of friends. We get along great. So, when we saw this was available we agreed that we'd have a look. We decided if we liked it, we'd give it a try."

Slave Quarters

Marge spoke up from the far end of the table and added, "When we agreed to look at the place, we came down with the owner. She's an older woman in her 80s who hadn't lived down here in 25 years. She insisted that we see it before the renters, who had been in here for 15 years, moved out. That way, we could ask them any questions we wanted about the house. At the time, I wished we didn't, but in the end it was a good thing we did."

Why, I wondered.

"Because," Susan replied, eager to share her thoughts on this topic, "the place was a complete disaster. It was absolutely horrible, almost uninhabitable—trash everywhere, broken windows with plastic over them to keep out the wind. Sometimes I wonder how we could see the potential that was hidden beneath all the mess and garbage. But," she added, proudly looking around at the brick fireplace and recently exposed original plaster walls, "as you can see, we didn't do a bad job. And we're still at it."

Marge described the house on their first walk through as "horrifying." But she stressed she knew it had potential. There was one strange incident that occurred in the kitchen. At the time, she said it did not seem worth noting. However, more than 18 months of ghostly encounters later, the two women agreed they should have realized that something out of the ordinary was afoot.

Susan said the renters had closed off the back stairway in the kitchen that led up to the servants' quarters.

"It wasn't just barricaded with boxes," Susan recalled, "it was actually nailed shut at the top and bottom. When I realized there were rooms up there, I told the owner that I wanted to go up and see the rooms for myself. The woman who lived here, the renter, definitely didn't want me to go up there. But I insisted. We waited in the kitchen and watched while she moved away the boxes and then used a claw hammer to pry the nails out in order to get the door to open."

Marge added, "While Susan went up and looked around, the renter woman turned to me and said, 'We never go up there. Don't ever want to. The children are afraid of it up there.' And the children," Marge said, shaking her head, "were 17 and 19 years old. That gave me the willies."

Explaining that records indicate that the farmhouse was built around 1750, Susan said they probably had slaves in the building. If so, some of them may have lived in the tiny rooms above the kitchen. Also, a few local residents told Susan and Marge that the tunnel from the kitchen is believed to be a part of the Underground Railroad.

"If this was a safe house for slaves," Susan said, "that might explain the sounds of a baby crying and footsteps that you can hear from the servants area when you are in the kitchen or dining room. And that room upstairs, above the kitchen, is eerie. There also have been the sounds of chains rattling from this area. I don't know why, but I've heard them."

Sighting in the Cellar

While the noises above the kitchen may grab a visitor's attention, it's the apparition of the old black lady in the cellar, directly below the kitchen, that Susan finds most fascinating.

"I come down to wash clothes a few times a week, and quite a few of those times I've seen her standing in the same spot, in the corner, looking down at the ground," Susan said. "She has an apron on around her waist and a bandanna on her head. To me she looks just like Aunt Jemima. That's what I call her—Aunt Jemima."

I asked how many times Susan had seen the old woman.

"Frequently," she said without hesitation. "More at night. At least a dozen times. I talk to her, tell her I'm here and I want to help. I stare right at her, and after a few moments I'll turn my head

and look back and she's gone. I think she's just making herself
known. I get a very warm feeling. I look for her and hope she's
here. None of this scares me. They've been here longer than I've
been here. I don't believe they mean us any harm, and I think they
know we feel the same about them."

Then there's Uncle Ned.

Laughing, Marge pointed toward a section in the dining room
beside the fireplace. "That's where he appeared," the older woman
said, adding that the ghost has been described as an old fellow
dressed like a farmer and wearing black suspenders. The first wit-
ness was Susan's three-year-old nephew who was visiting during a
special open house for family members in the spring of 1998.

"Little Tommy," Susan said, "was standing in the archway
between the living room and dining room when he said, 'Look!
There's a man standing next to the wall!' "

According to Marge, "That got everybody's attention. It was
real to him. Then Tommy said, 'It looks like the man is playing
with his hat!' Well, people turned white. Half realized Tommy was
talking about a ghost, and the other half were totally shocked and
didn't know what to believe. There was no one else standing near
that area. There were about 18 people here at the time, but there
were a lot fewer in the house right after Tommy started pointing
to that corner of the room. Several of our guests said they had to
go right away."

"I saw him, Uncle Ned, too," Susan added. "I was sitting on
the couch one night and looked over toward the dining room fireplace and he was right there. He didn't remain that long. He
looked like a picture in the real old movies, not real solid, but not
completely transparent. But he didn't bother me."

Visions for Visitors

Apparently, the ghosts in the old farmhouse don't restrict
their activities to times when the owners are home alone. These
spirits seem to enjoy grabbing the attention of visitors as well.

One evening, Jake, a friend of the family, was sleeping
overnight on the living room couch. He had to be at work very
early, at 4:30 in the morning, but had forgotten to set an alarm.

"All of the sudden," Jake said, "I heard this crashing sound,
like pots and pans had fallen on the kitchen floor. It was loud
enough that I shot up and it had my heart pumping. I got up, ran

21

into the kitchen to see what fell on the floor . . . and there was nothing. Nothing at all. But, the clock said 4:31. I swear, I got up, got dressed and hotfooted it out of here real fast."

Both Marge and Susan heard the crashing noise from upstairs, ran down to investigate and found nothing out of place. The cause of the loud crash remains another mystery that the old house has not yet decided to share.

"We find pennies," Marge said, shaking her head, "and dimes, too. Sometimes they're on the floor, in the corners of the rooms, and always with their heads up. At first, I thought it was money falling out of our pockets. But it was impossible. We checked. Also, the money shows up on the edge of the washing machine, in the basement."

"And they're all lined up in a straight line," Susan said, "and face up. Sometime it happens once a week. It's been going on for quite a while."

Marge has found coins in the spare room while cleaning, even when they have not had any guests or visitors. "They even have appeared inside the fireplaces," she added.

Susan said she has to get up early for work. Often, the thumping of footsteps and the sound of piano music, apparently coming from the music room, disturbs her rest.

"When I can't take it anymore," she said, smiling, "I yell, 'This is not funny! I've got to get some rest before I go to work. You guys are not funny. Why don't you do it during the day?' And then they'll quiet down and leave me alone for a while."

In addition to footsteps, indecipherable whispers and rattling chains, Susan and Marge have noticed that doors will be open after they have been latched shut. Items, which the women place in certain spots, will disappear and reappear later—in the same site or in other locations.

The piano music is intriguing. "It sounds like a kid trying to learn to play the piano," Susan said. "The kid is hitting notes, but it's not a recognizable song. Sometimes, when I hear it in the middle of the night, I slip out of bed, leave the lights off and sneak down to the first floor. The minute I reach my hand into the music room and hit the light switch, the light blazes and the music stops. That's when I say, 'I know you're here!' "

There's also the sticky piano key story.

Susan explained that one key on the piano stays down if it is played. Often, she will be sure the key is upright before she goes to bed. Then, when she checks in the morning, the key is depressed.

Calm Conversations

Susan also talks to the ghosts.

"I'm comfortable with them," she said. "If someone is coming that I know fears the unknown, I tell them not to act up. I told them you were coming and invited them to appear or do some-thing noticeable while you were here. I told them they were going to be in a book. Nothing's happened yet, but the day's still young."

I smiled, quickly looking around the room for a sign.

Marge's most unusual incident occurred when she was stand-ing on a stepladder pulling staples out of the window frames that had been covered with shredded plastic.

While working alone in the room several feet above the ground, Marge heard a soft voice say, "Be careful."

"It was just as clear as day," Marge recalled, adding that she thought Susan was calling out from the other room, teasing her. Thinking she would surprise her daughter, Marge stepped off the ladder, crept down the hall and looked around for her daughter. But Susan was outside, unloading the car. No one else had been inside the house with Marge.

Shaking her head, Marge returned to her job, climbing the ladder and pulling out a few more staples, when she cut the tip of one of her fingers. As she sucked a drop of blood off the end of her finger, Marge heard the same voice say, "I told you to be careful."

"This voice," Marge recalled, "was just as clear as the first time. It was a female voice. I got down off the ladder again, and looked around for Susan. She was still outside. That made me a believer for the rest of my life."

A few weeks later, an electrician was working on an outlet near the edge of the living room doorway that led into the main entry hall. For some reason, he happened to peer around the edge of the wall and saw a woman dressed in old-fashioned farm clothing sitting on the steps that led to the second floor.

Marge said, "The electrician said the woman looked at him and said, 'I'll be out of the way in a minute.' The man nodded, started to resume his work and then realized something was very strange. He looked back around the corner again and the ghost woman was gone. He told me, 'I leaned back and said to myself— I'm out of here!' He got up, left the wire, tool and wall plate by that outlet, and he didn't go back to fix it for three days. Later, he told me, 'After what I saw, I wasn't coming back, ever.' "

Laughing at the thought of the conversation and the look on the man's face, Marge said she told him the ghosts were friendly and wouldn't hurt him.

Apparently, Marge and Susan's ghosts also are protective of the new owners.

One Sunday, a relative known for her loud and vulgar language was expected to visit. When the young lady, known as Kate, entered the home, Susan cautioned her about cursing and using four-letter words. Within 15 minutes, while walking through the music room, Kate began to swear aloud. Suddenly, a candle, that was sitting inside a glass holder, leapt straight up, exited the container, turned, flew four feet across the room and hit Kate on the shoulder.

"Kate started screaming and yelling," Susan recalled. "She went out on the porch and refused to come back into the house. I told her that she had been warned and that the ghosts didn't like the way she talked. She hasn't been back since."

"I think the ghosts are protective of us," Marge said, looking across the table at Susan, who nodded, agreeing with her mother.

Once, after Susan and her boyfriend had been having an argument, something pushed the man forward and knocked him down as he was walking up the stairs.

"It was with such force," Susan said, "that it caused his chest to hit against the steps. But when he looked around there was no one anywhere near him. He figured they didn't like the way he was shouting at me."

For Marge and Susan, unusual or unexplained incidents seem to occur frequently.

"Things happen so often," Susan said, "that I don't think much about them anymore. I don't find myself pausing and noticing them. But I'm not afraid. In fact, I've never been afraid. What I always say is, 'It's the living that can hurt you.' I'm comfortable. I feel like we have family here. We're never alone."

Pets and Coffee

Her pet rabbit, Buster, who lives in a cage in the living room seems to be tamer since moving into the farmhouse.

The pet used to be agitated, Marge said. "Maybe he's getting the attention he needs during the night from someone that he can see and we can't. You hear a lot of noises associated with the cages at night. It's probably the rabbit moving around. But maybe it's something else. Who knows?"

"One of the things I like is the smell of coffee in the morning," Marge said. "And that happens a lot of times."

"Except," Susan added, "there is no coffee, which is disturbing, actually. If I can smell it, why can't it be here?"

Marge said she's gotten to the point where she walks into a room or section of the house and expects to find someone other than her daughter there.

"At one time, we had wanted to have the house blessed," Susan said. "But then we realized that a ritual might actually cause the spirits to leave. Since we were afraid to chase them away, we decided not to call the priest and just leave things alone. I feel very safe in our home, and I feel special— that whoever is here has chosen for us to see them, for us to know that they are here."

"Maybe that's because the house is coming back to life," Marge suggested. "It's brighter now than it was when we came here. It's warm, friendly, inviting. We have curtains. It's like there's life in the house now. I think this house is happy again."

For Susan, the haunted home is a dream come true. "I've always wanted an old house. Oddly, my dream came true. I came to see it, and I felt it needed someone to take care of it. It needed work, but me and Mom have got a lot done. There's still a lot to do, too."

And probably a lot more to discover.

'I Believe That Story'

M ary lives in Dover and believes in ghosts. Her husband, Bob, is a skeptic. "I don't believe any of this stuff," he said. "It's fun to read, but that's all there is to it. The only things I believe are when they happen to me."

Eventually, the sprits seem to have singled Bob out for special attention.

Several years ago, Mary and Bob went to Clearwater, Florida, to visit Mary's sister, Jane, who lived in a beautiful old mansion with a wrap-around porch, stained glass windows and two turrets overlooking the sea.

The home was part of an expensive resort, located on a small island. A large hotel was nearby, but Jane's husband, who was the hotel manager, lived with his family in the nearby mansion that was built by a rich merchant in the early 1800s.

One day Mary was alone in the house while everyone else was out shopping or running errands. She had been sitting by the pool, enjoying the warm sun, when she decided to go inside to the upstairs guest room and get her cigarettes.

"I remember entering the room, which was beautifully decorated with fine antiques, plush carpets and attractive wallpaper," she said, "and every hair on my body jumped up. I just froze. It was like I was inside a freezer, it was so cold, and I couldn't move—not an inch. I remember saying with my mind, 'Feet get me out of here.' As soon as I got outside that room, I ran out of

the house and I sat near the pool until someone else came home.
I would not go back inside. I'll never forget what it was like. That
was a horrible feeling. That room was as cold as ice, but I didn't
see anything."

Later during the visit, Mary learned that one of her nephews
said he loved to play in that room because, "There is a beautiful
lady, all dressed in a blue dress, that keeps me company."

Another story associated with the haunted house, as Mary now
calls it, involved her niece, who was reprimanded at dinner for
scraping her fork against her plate, causing an annoying sound.

"Her parents told her to stop it, but she said she wasn't doing
anything," Mary recalled. "So, out of the corner of their eyes, my
sister and her husband looked very carefully in the girl's direction
the next time the sound occurred. And," Mary paused, "they said
they saw their daughter's fork, on its own, moving in the air, scrap-
ping its prongs against her plate."

One year, Mary and Bob stayed in the home themselves, for a
private Florida vacation, while her sister's family was away.

"We were there all alone," Mary said. "We made sure every
window and door was locked up tight each night, and whenever we
left the house during the day. We were careful. After all, it wasn't
our home and we wanted to treat it properly. One night, we were
awakened by strange sounds coming from inside the walls.

"I put on the light and woke up Bob. Together, sitting in bed,
we heard heavy, distinct footsteps coming down the hall toward
our room. But there was no exposed wood on the second level.
The floors had been covered with thick, expensive carpeting. Then,
the doorknob started to turn. But since it was locked, it could only
move so far back and forth. Bob jumped up, grabbed a stick or
club of some type, unlocked the door and yanked it open. But
there was no one out there.

"I wouldn't let him leave the room and check the rest of the
house. We stayed up all night, with the lights on, and didn't get
any sleep. The next morning, we both went downstairs, together.
We checked every room and window. But, just like we left things
the night before, they all were locked up tightly. That was the
scariest thing I ever experienced.

"I told my one daughter about it. Then next time she went
down to visit, she made it a point to go into that room. She said it
felt like a refrigerator in there."

The house is gone now, Mary said. It was torn down when the hotel expanded. She said she knows the exact site of where it once stood, not far from the end of the small bridge that carries travelers onto the island.

But, Mary added, her sister shared a legend associated with the haunted mansion. It's said there was a wealthy man who married his sweetheart, who he had met in the Carolinas. He returned to Florida alone and promised to send for her as soon as the special house he was building was completed.

While standing in the window, in the tower of their new home, waiting for her to arrive, the man saw her ship approach from the north. However, his excitement turned to terror as, within sight of land, he helplessly watched her ship catch fire. Everyone aboard perished, including his young bride.

I knew what Mary thought about ghosts, so I turned to Bob and asked him to explain his feelings about the Florida home—and spirits in general.

"Hey," he said. "There were strange things going on in there. Footsteps. Lights would go on and off by themselves. Wind would blow through the room like there was a storm, but there was nothing open and it was calm outside. That place was something else."

So, I asked, are you a believer, now?

"I believe that story!" he said, smiling. "I don't know about all the other stuff she reads, but I believe that story."

Moving a Body
for Fun and Profit

While this is not a ghost story, I believe it is appropriate since it has to do with what happened to a person that I met immediately after his death. Everything described in this story actually happened. The names of those involved and the exact location where it occurred have been changed, even though Doc's place is long gone and a different type of business now operates out of the old neighborhood funeral parlor site. I can honestly say, that this unusual event has been branded in my mind and in the memory of the real "Stan," who helped me carry a dead body into Doc's place.

One summer years ago, my Delaware family was visiting the coal-mining country of central Pennsylvania. It was a small village where my grandfather had settled in the early 1900s after he had arrived from Poland and made it through Ellis Island. I still have relatives who live in the small gray towns that project from the side of the pit-scarred mountains like Plasticville train platform villages.

As we did during previous visits, we spent most of our time sitting on the screened back porch, talking about the days when coal was king and the town was really jumping. My uncles and aunts were full of stories which entertain me as much as they do my children. And they get better each time we hear them.

There's one thing about small-town America that is definitely missing in our larger urban/suburban areas—an eagerness to help your neighbor when he is in need, no matter what the request.

One sweltering afternoon as my cousin Stan and I shared a brew on the porch, feeling stuffed after a hot, home-cooked lunch of pierogies, sauerkraut and kielbasa, my aunt announced that the man next door needed a hand. Stan, a hefty plumbing contractor, popped up like a piece of toast and motioned for me to follow. No questions asked—just head on out and lend a hand. But as I approached the back door of the house next door, tiny floating question marks began flashing in the back of my head.

It started when my eyes zeroed in on the two Cadillac hearses, sparkling like matched pieces of black onyx in the oversize garage. But on the way over, my cousin had promised some quick money for about 10 minutes' work. Who was I to question his judgment?

Slowly the door to the residence opened and a tall, cadaverous creature stepped down into the garage. If someone wanted to depict the ultimate undertaker, this would be the man: tall, emaciated, black-suited, sporting a waxed silver mane and, of course, a cold clammy handshake.

Dr. Kloftt led us to the rear of one of his black beauties. Inside, wrapped in a bright yellow blanket, was . . . the remains.

"It's just some old fella I happened to pick up on the way home for lunch," the good doctor said, nonchalantly.

Stan just nodded; I nodded, too.

I was beginning to wonder what the local good-neighbor policy had gotten me into.

"I want to take him 'round to the front door and into the parlor, boys," said Doc. "Got his sister comin' in to see him first thing tomorrow, so it's a rush job."

Our host slid the stretcher out of the rear of the hearse, motioning us to grab the sides. The wheels on Doc's end fell to the street automatically, giving him some support. The front wheels stayed folded up, and the two of us— facing one anoth-er—clutched the sides of the stainless steel stretcher near the dear departed's lifeless head.

Stan had to strain to keep his side upright. I was using all my strength to do the same. The nameless dead guy weighed a ton and a half—I don't know if it had something to do with the term "dead weight." Sweat dripped from my forehead onto the yellow blanket.

"How about putting down our wheels, Doc?" asked my cousin.

"Not now!" Kloftt snapped. "Keep moving. Can't stop in midstream."

With great difficulty, we dragged, we sagged, we juggled the stretcher and the mound of flesh it held down the slanted, irregular front sidewalk leading to the entrance steps of Kloftt's Funeral Home.

Cars were stopping at the red light on the corner. Drivers tooted their horns and waved in delight as we stumbled toward our goal.

"Hurry up!" ordered the Doc. "Don't want the whole world watchin'." His voice had the tone of a Puritan clergyman giving orders at a witch trial.

We tried to rush. The useless gurney teetered.

"I don't think I can make it," groaned my cousin, his biceps bulging from the weight.

As we struggled down the sidewalk in the midday sun, I noticed that the blanket was beginning to fall off our cargo's face.

"Stan," I hissed through the pain, "the cover's falling. He's looking up at me."

"Damn!" Stan said, "I don't want to look at him. Hell, Doc!" Stan shouted at the undertaker, "the damn blanket's falling off. I can see the bastard's face."

"Ignore it!" Doc ordered. "He can't see you. He's gone. Just don't pay him any mind. Just do your job."

"Do my job?" Stan shouted. "I can't if he's staring at me like this."

Suddenly, a passing motorist rolled down his truck window and yelled, "How much of a discount is it without a hearse?"

Even the squeal of the pickup's rubber didn't drown out the driver's roaring laughter. Obviously, the Doc had a well-deserved reputation for cutting corners.

Stan had endured enough.

"Let's hit it!" he shouted, and the two of us took off in a mad effort to crash into the funeral parlor lobby. We must have looked like an aging team of mortuary college fraternity brothers, dragging our stretcher toward the finish line.

But this was no spring-fling keg race. This was real world deceased delivery in small-town America.

In the lead, the two of us—in cutoff jeans, sweat-drenched T-shirts and dirty sneakers—dragged the gurney at top speed.

31

Bringing up the rear was an 85-year-old Ichabod Crane, dressed in his finest mourning regalia. And along for the bumpiest ride of his "life" was our recently departed, grossly overweight coal miner.

Dr. Kloftt's bride, who looked like one of the undertaker's early experiments that failed, waited on the threshold. As we vaulted up the three steps toward the paradise of the funeral parlor's interior and relief, the "missis" opened the storm door and in we rushed.

Once we were settled inside the main parlor, Doc reached over, hit a button under the middle of the gurney, and the wheels on our side of the stainless steel chariot snapped down and hit the floor. Finally, able to release our death grip, we moaned as we relaxed our burning arms.

Stepping back, we noticed the yellow blanket had fallen to the floor, revealing the entire body of our nameless traveler. The dead man's face was set in a menacing scowl, and his puffy fat hands were facing up, like open claws. I imagined he wanted to grab the throats of the two idiots who had been tossing him around on the open stretcher.

Obviously relieved that our chore was done, and that we were out of view from passers-by on the main drag, Doc mopped his brow with a white silk handkerchief and the smiling missis dispensed the pay. Pressing a $5 bill into my hand and then Stan's, she whispered her thanks and invited us to dinner, which was set on the kitchen table within three feet of the deceased. In one voice, Stan and I declined.

"Would you boys be available in two days to serve as *paid* pallbearers for the funeral?" Doc asked. "Since ya already know the departed. Plus, there's another fiver in it for each of ya," he added.

With false reluctance, we passed up that invitation, too.

After we walked back into my cousin's house, we sank into my aunt's living room chairs and howled with laughter. Did this sort of thing happen often, I wondered.

"Not really," Stan said, "only every time the Doc gets a funeral."

"Every time?" I asked with surprise.

"Right," Stan said. "That's about twice a year, and worth every minute of the fun. And you can see why I was glad you were here, 'cause you wouldn't have believed me if you didn't see all this for yourself."

The Lore and Lure of Lighthouses

There's an enchantment associated with lighthouses that goes far beyond the appeal of their physical appearance. While artists and photographers use these towers as subjects of paintings and pictures, others are fascinated by the lore of these silent sentinels perched on the edge of the sea. Even vacant lights, whose beams have been extinguished and cold for decades, still have the power to lure vacationers and locals, much like their beaming predecessors seized the attention of sailors and ships for centuries.

Since the earliest days of our country, when the sea was the primary means of passenger travel and commerce, the need for a series of coastal lighthouses was evident. Blazing beacons guided incoming vessels safely into unknown harbors and marked geographic points of interest. Eventually, they became sought after points of conquest during the battle for American independence.

History, Local Lights and Preservation

This continent's first lighthouse-like structure, Boston Light, was a wooden tower with a fire tended upon its top. It was erected in 1716 on Little Brewster Island in Massachusetts. Like many of the earliest colonial lighthouses, its need was recognized and demanded by merchants who petitioned local courts and the government. Boston Light's original structure was damaged by fire in 1751 and blown up by the British in 1776. The present tower was built in 1859 and still stands 89 feet above its base.

Delaware can proudly claim its role in the country's extensive lighthouse history as site of one of the very earliest U.S. lighthouses built in 1767 at Cape Henlopen. The stone tower was constructed at the request of Philadelphia traders and businessmen. However, it was built upon a sandy foundation. In the spring of 1926, after years of erosion and wind, the sea claimed the historic light structure and it toppled over.

Today, scores of Lewes area residents proudly point out that the stones used to build their fireplaces were salvaged from the Cape Henlopen Light. Sandy Hook Light Station, a similar-shaped lighthouse built in 1764 along New Jersey's northern Atlantic Coast, is still in operation and today is considered the nation's oldest operating lighthouse.

Maryland didn't get its first light station until the beginning of the 19th century. In 1802, a light was established at Smith Point, at the entrance of the Potomac River. It took several decades for more lights to be added in the Chesapeake Bay, with installations established in the Upper Bay at Pooles Island and Thomas Point in the mid-1820s. In the 1830s, mariners saw the addition of Point Lookout at the entrance of the Potomac River; Turkey Point, south of North East, Maryland; and Sharps Island, at the mouth of the Choptank River. Assateague Island Light—located on the popular barrier island known as Chincoteague National Wildlife Refuge and east of the village of Chincoteague, Virginia—was first erected in 1833. Since that area of the Atlantic Coast was a considered dangerous for shipping, the intensity of this light was improved in later years.

According to Alan Ross, in his book *The Lure of Lighthouses*, the Delaware Bay's Brandywine Shoal Light, built in 1850, is the country's oldest "screw pile" lighthouse. These structures used wide, screw-like blades, which twisted the pilings into the sand and coral to anchor the foundation.

In a book entitled *America's Lighthouses* by Francis Ross Holland Jr., in 1877, Ship John Shoal Light—named after a vessel *John* that sank at the site in 1797—was erected in Delaware Bay. This is a caisson-base structure—which uses a concrete-filled, cast iron cylinder as its foundation. Fourteen Foot Bank Lighthouse, another Delaware Bay caisson-base light, was completed and lighted in 1887. A standing lighthouse that today is almost obscured by modern development is Fenwick Island Light. Built in 1858, it rises 83 feet above the sea, and it stands practically along a portion of the Mason-Dixon Line that separates the southern boundary of Delaware from the northern coastal line of Maryland.

Since their beginnings lighthouses were tended or "manned" around the clock, every day of the year. Sometimes this was done for several generations by members of the same family, who were employed by the Bureau of Lighthouses and later by the U.S. Coast Guard. Stories and legends are told of the effects of months of desolation at lonely rocky outposts, faithfully tending the light while battling the weather and the sea. Lighthouse keepers have died tending their lights, been lost at sea during travels to and from the mainland and, in several cases, been credited with the rescue of humans and animals that were victims of nearby shipwrecks and accidents on the water.

While the work was hard and isolation difficult, the romance associated with the life of the lighthouse keeper has reached a level today where it rivals the legends of the Wild West cowboy and the exploits of the seafaring pirate. How much is true and how much is folklore is hard to determine and, in the end, the precise answers are of little interest, for lighthouses are the theme of enchantment.

Unfortunately, as time progressed, technological advances changed the management of the lights while the forces of the sea affected the survival of the structures. Today, the lighthouse keepers are gone—replaced by automated lights, which are considered more dependable and cheaper to employ. Blazing lights, operated by mini computer chips and high-tech devices, alert ships to coastal landmarks and hazards near shore. At the same time, the power of the waves, which attack foundations and shorelines with never-ending regularity—and the forces of weather that affect the wood and stone structures themselves—threaten the maintenance and very existence of many vacant lighthouses.

In recent years, individuals and preservationist groups have saved many lighthouses from ruin and destruction caused by inattention, decay and misuse. In nearby Maryland, the Hooper Straight Lighthouse was automated in 1954 and the building declared surplus by the U.S. Coast Guard. The Chesapeake Bay Maritime Museum, located 60 miles to the north in St. Michaels, Maryland, had the lighthouse building dismantled and barged up the Chesapeake Bay. The structure was restored in 1967. Now, at the edge of the dock in a popular resort town on the Eastern Shore, thousands of visitors a year walk through this distinctive, octagonal-shaped structure— built in 1867—and are able to gain a glimpse of its historic past.

Cape Hatteras Light has been located on North Carolina's Outer Banks since the original structure was built in 1803. During the summer of 1999, the current tower, which was built in 1870, was moved nearly 3,000 feet inland to avoid being toppled by erosion. At 193 feet, it is the country's tallest lighthouse and the preservation effort cost nearly $10 million. This move insured that the structure, bearing its distinctive spiral, barber-pole, black-and-white stripes, will continue to signal ships that approach the Diamond Shoals—a dangerous rocky reef that extends more than 10 miles into the Atlantic Ocean. Because of the large number of shipwrecks in the area, the sea near this light has been called the Graveyard of the Atlantic.

Haunted Lights

Is there anything more eerie than a lighthouse at night, with its rhythmic flash projecting a bright beacon across the deep, dark, dangerous sea? One can only imagine the depths of terror, loneliness and isolation that the keepers and their families must have experienced. They were alone, surrounded by water and most certainly afraid of what might rise from the unknown deep. Some believe there is a resident ghost in every lighthouse.

Perhaps this is true, for there are scores of mysterious tales of phantom lights, ghostly keepers and invisible fog horns sounding through the thick mist of the sea.

One example occurred on Seguin Island, off the coast of southern Maine. A tower was lighted in 1797 and eventually rebuilt in 1857. The Lighthouse Board considered this area very important for East Coast shipping. Also, to dismiss persistent rumors that pirate treasure was buried somewhere on the island, it's said that the Bureau of Lighthouses hired a man to dig on the island for one full year in an effort to find the lost treasure. He was unsuccessful.

A most eerie, haunted tale associated with **Seguin Island Light** involves the sound of a recurring song played by the lighthouse keeper's wife on a piano that her husband had ordered delivered to their residence on the secluded island.

Because the instrument arrived with only one selection of sheet music, it's said the wife played the same melody over and over, until it was carried on the winds and reached the ears of those living on the mainland. After some time, the music stopped. A later visit to the keeper on the island found that the husband had killed his wife and destroyed the piano with an ax and then committed suicide. It's believed the sound of the repetitive music drove him mad. Subsequent lighthouse keepers have written in their logs, and passing boaters have reported, that they have heard the repeated sounds of the familiar piano melody.

St. Simons Light, a coastal light located on St. Simons Island east of Brunswick, Georgia, was built in 1857. During the Civil War Confederate soldiers destroyed the cottage and tower. In 1872 a new light in the replacement tower was back in operation. However, there is a story that an argument occurred on the island in the early 1880s between the keeper and his assistant over the affections of the keeper's wife. The fight resulted in the lighthouse keeper's death. It's said the spirit of the murdered man still walks the metal steps of the Georgia island light tower.

St. Augustine Light, first built in the new territory of Florida in 1821, was destroyed by Rebel soldiers during the Civil War and relighted in 1867. Because of erosion, a new tower was constructed in 1872 and lit in 1874. Over the years, and even during more recent times, there have been reports of sightings of phantom lighthouse keepers and a 12-year-old little girl.

Point Lookout Light

What some consider "the most haunted lighthouse in America" stands at Point Lookout, Maryland. Although it is now empty and surrounded by a rusted chain link fence—and is only open to the public for a mere four hours on one day of the year—tales of its spirits and other strange activities throughout the area around the lighthouse persist.

To understand the reasons behind ghostly activity around Point Lookout, one must realize that the land now known as Point Lookout State Park had been the site of the "nation's largest Civil War prison," housing more than 52,000 Confederate prisoners during the War of Northern Aggression or as the Yankees called it—the Civil War. (Please see the following chapter on Point Lookout State Park, the Nation's Largest Civil War Prison, for complete details on the history of this haunted and historic region.)

According to Donnie Hammett, assistant park manager of Point Lookout State Park, there are a significant number of ghost stories associated with the lighthouse. Some have been featured on such popular television programs as *In Search Of* . . . , *Strange Universe* and *Haunted Lighthouses*. Psychics, authors, historians and relatives of Confederate and Union solders have visited the park and historic sites seeking answers and stories.

But it is around and in the lighthouse, built in 1830 and located at the southernmost tip of Maryland's Western Shore, where much ghostly activity occurs.

To respond to frequent requests for information about the park's ghosts and legends, the Point Lookout Camp Host Volunteers organization, under the direction of Ralph and Judy Bloor, recently compiled a pamphlet entitled *True Tales of the Bizarre and Unnatural at Point Lookout*. Some of the following incidents have been summarized from that publication with permission.

Mysterious Activity at the Lighthouse

In the park pamphlet, Hammett said, "Nearly everyone who has lived in the Point Lookout Lighthouse had reported hearing footsteps coming from empty corridors. The mysterious footsteps are so commonplace they are seldom given notice anymore."

The lighthouse is a duplex structure with two mirror-like dwellings that stand side by side and are separated by a common wall. At the top of the building is the cupola of the Point Lookout Light. Hammett said numerous reports of strange footsteps have been made by past residents. He explained that those living on one side of the building have said they hear footsteps coming from the living quarters on the opposite side of the building. Also, these sounds always were reported as coming from the second floor.

But, Hammett said, "They have never been explained."

Hammett recalled that Park Manager Gerry Sword, who is now deceased, resided in the north side of the lighthouse. At night, Mr. Sword would put his German Shepherd on the building's west porch, which stands about six feet above the ground and was completely screened in. At night, the porch door was latched from the inside, but one morning Mr. Sword awoke and found his dog running around on the lighthouse lawn. He checked the porch and discovered that a section of screen had been pushed down from the outside and was laying inside the porch. There had been no wind and the dog would have barked if it had seen an intruder.

Later, Mr. Sword moved to a home on the park that was adjacent to an old Civil War road that ran the length of Point Lookout. He said his German Shepherd seemed to stop and "see" someone or something traveling along the old road. Other times the dog would bark and lunge against its chain, as if trying to reach an invisible intruder passing along the road.

According to the park pamphlet, Mr. Sword had told a lady who was moving into the lighthouse about his experiences while he was a resident in the building. Mr. Sword said he would hear snoring in the kitchen and voices outside the back of the house and in the front yard, too. But when he went to check, no one was there. One evening, Mr. Sword said he saw figures of men going through the house, but the sight was never able to be explained.

This new lighthouse resident was known to have had several encounters while living in the building. On her first night in the structure, the woman reported that she was awakened by the sound of heavy boots walking down the hall. She also discovered that one of the rooms had a very bad odor at night. Sometimes, she said she heard the sound of a woman's voice singing at the top of the stairs. She also heard men's voices in the living room and once saw two figures in the basement.

Some friends who visited the woman and stayed as guests at the lighthouse also reported unusual experiences. One friend said she saw a lady in a blue dress standing in the living room.

One of the strangest experiences was when the lighthouse resident was awakened by an unusual series of six lights. Getting up, she looked outside to determine the origin, but there was no car in the area and no boat on the water. Then she smelled smoke, went to investigate, and found that her space heater was on fire. Alerted by the unknown lights, she was able to put out the fire, which would have done serious damage to the building.

Another lighthouse resident told about the night he was fixing dinner in the kitchen and the wall began to glow. The brightness started as a spot the size of a dinner plate and gradually increased until it was four feet across. After a few minutes, the glow faded away. No explanation has ever been found.

Hammett's sister, Anne, who lived in the lighthouse one summer while working as a seasonal park employee, reported seeing a woman standing at the foot of her bed. She said there was no question in her mind that the figure was that of an older lady. Anne later learned that one of her former elementary school classmates, who had lived in the same room in the lighthouse when she was younger, had been visited in the same room. Shortly after Anne's young friend's grandmother's death, members of her family discovered the young girl talking with her deceased grandmother in the middle of the night—in the same room where Anne had seen the apparition.

Anne and Donnie Hammett's brother, Mark, who lived in the lighthouse building a different summer, was outside and noticed lights coming from the lighthouse's darkened interior. He and other workers followed the beams of lights through several rooms and, finally, up into the top floor of the lighthouse, thinking they would catch the intruder. But, when they cornered the light source in the last room, from which it couldn't escape, the room was empty.

George Steitz, writer and producer of several television documentaries, said he made a number of visits to Point Lookout State Park while filming his program *Haunted Lighthouses*. We met in the spring of 1999, during his stop at Fort Delaware, where he produced a segment about the island prison's hauntings for his program *Ghost Waters*.

"Lighthouses," Steitz told me, "are romantic and spiritual places. They evoke a sense of history, especially in America where they seem to be our answer to Europe's castles. But are any of them haunted? Many people certainly think so, and I talked with dozens of them in the making of *Haunted Lighthouses* and the follow-up show, *Ghost Waters*.

"I did not see or hear any ghosts myself. The closest I came to a supernatural experience was a strange and unsettling feeling I had at Point Lookout Lighthouse. I can't explain it because I don't think we have words to accurately describe this type of experience. At another location someone once commented that in certain places there may be rips or holes in time through which we can sense activity in another dimension, one inhabited by what we call ghosts. I thought about this at Point Lookout. It may in fact be a genuinely haunted lighthouse."

The Nation's Largest Civil War Prison

On a clear December day, I headed south for a three-and-a-half-hour drive to one of the country's most haunted sites—Point Lookout State Park, located at the bottom tip of Maryland's Western Shore.

For years readers had been sharing fascinating stories of ghostly activity and unexplained incidents reported at this well-known historical site. After years of occasional phone conversations with Assistant Park Manager Donnie Hammett and Park Ranger Kevin Hook—and reading several books about the colorful history of this southern Maryland region—I was finally on my way.

When I arrived, I took a quick drive through the park. As I passed through dense forests, stopped for a quick look at the famous haunted lighthouse, walked around the buildings and over the ramparts of Fort Lincoln and looked out at the Chesapeake Bay to my left and the mouth of the Potomac River to my right, one word came to mind that would accurately describe this area—isolated.

Standing at "the point," which is, literally the end of the Earth, surrounded on three sides by the sea, one can immediately understand why the Union decided that Point Lookout would be an excellent site for a prison to hold captured Confederate soldiers. For it was, and apparently still is, impossible for their bodies and spirits to escape from this haunted and hallowed ground.

History

In 1634, two ships, the *Ark* and the *Dove*, landed north of the sandy point with 200 passengers, and Maryland's first settlement was established at St. Mary's City. In coming years, more colonists arrived in the region and settled on land at what was called St. Michaels Point. Today, the area is known as Point Lookout. Since the first arrival of the white settlers, there was trouble with the American Indians, and there are reports that several colonists were massacred by these natives.

Point Lookout Light was built in 1830 at the southernmost tip of the state's Western Shore. The building now stands in Point Lookout State Park, which was established in 1965. Over the years, the point's ownership changed hands. By the time the Civil War (War of Northern Aggression) began in 1861, the point was a resort area with a hotel and about 100 beach cottages.

A year after the start of the war, the U.S. government leased the bottom tip of the Maryland peninsula to establish a military hospital to treat members of the Northern armies who needed medical care. From 1863-1865 this isolated region—surrounded by the waters of the Potomac River and Chesapeake Bay—became the site of the "nation's largest Civil War prison," housing more than 52,000 Confederate prisoners during its two-year period.

It is important to understand that residents of this geographical area of Maryland—like others throughout the vast majority of the state—were sympathetic to the Southern cause and secession. St. Mary's County had established militia units that were preparing to fight for the Confederacy as soon as the state formally seceded. But, if Maryland left the Union, Washington City, the U.S. capital, would have been surrounded by hostile Rebel territory—namely Virginia and Maryland. To solve this problem, Maryland Gov. Hicks used political maneuvering, and President Abraham Lincoln used federal force and invaded the state. Eventually, Maryland's legislators were forced to vote against secession and, on paper, Maryland remained a loyal member of the United State.

However, a large number of the Free State's residents remained opposed to the Union cause. Their sons demonstrated their beliefs by escaping from Maryland and heading into Virginia to fight in that state's military units against the Yankees.

Today, graves of Maryland's Confederate soldiers can be found throughout the state, and one is located in a cemetery on Main Street in Elkton, Maryland, one of Maryland's northernmost counties.

It should be of no surprise that St. Mary's County residents were concerned for the Confederate prisoners who were under guard at Point Lookout Prison. Repeatedly, area citizens tried to deliver food, blankets and supplies to help the prisoners. However, these requests were often denied by Union commanders under strict orders from Edwin M. Stanton, Lincoln's secretary of war, who loathed the South and all of its citizens and supporters.

Haunts

According to Donnie Hammett, assistant park manager of Point Lookout State Park, there are about 30 ghost stories concerning unusual incidents associated with both the lighthouse and events at the former Civil War prison camp. He also mentioned that Point Lookout has been featured on such popular television programs as *In Search Of . . .* , *Strange Universe* and *Haunted Lighthouses*. Psychics, authors, historians and relatives of Confederate and Union solders have visited the park and historic sites seeking answers and stories. And, Hammett said, he gets several questions a month related to the ghosts at Point Lookout, and probably even one a day during the summer and fall.

There is so much unusual activity to share that The Point Lookout Camp Host Volunteers organization, under the direction of Ralph and Judy Bloor, recently compiled a pamphlet entitled *True Tales of the Bizarre and Unnatural at Point Lookout*. The 32-page booklet features stories that visitors have told to park personnel and other incidents have been experienced by members of the Point Lookout State Park staff. Several of these incidents that are presented in this chapter are summaries of material printed in the booklet and it is used with permission.

44

Dogs Can Tell

Humans are not the only creatures that have noticed peculiar episodes at the southern tip of the Maryland's Western Shore. Over the years, dogs, too, have perceived unusual activity at the Point Lookout Lighthouse, and these unexplained events have happened throughout the park grounds and in cottages and buildings occupied by Point Lookout employees.

A dog story reported in the park pamphlet tells of an animal owned by an assistant park manager who lived in a cottage on the park property. The employee would leave his dog inside its home during the workday. Apparently, the frightened animal was desperate to leave the building. At different times while the employee was at work, the dog jumped through several downstairs windows during numerous escape attempts. After each incident, the park employee replaced the damaged downstairs windows with Plexiglas.

This happened so often that, eventually, all the windows were repaired. One day, the dog jumped through a closed second-floor window, landed on the roof of an adjacent small porch, jumped onto the roof of a nearby car and then landed on the ground.

One wonders what could have frightened the dog.

* * * *

Kevin Hook, a park ranger at Point Lookout since 1992 told me he has lived in the same home on the park property. He admitted that, on certain nights, he believes he has heard what seems to be the sounds of prisoners walking outside, in a long column, along the old prison roads that they used more than 135 years ago.

He also said he has seen his dogs stare suddenly at certain spots in the room, where he and other humans that were present could not see anything. But the dogs continued to look at something that can't be seen.

"The house where I live lies adjacent to the main road where Confederate prisoners once marched on their way to be placed into the prison pen," he said.

The walls where the prison once stood are only 50 feet from Hook's home. "Looking out at the beautiful Chesapeake Bay," he said, "it's difficult to believe my backyard was the site of so much misery and suffering for 52,000 men during the Civil War."

One evening, Hook and two friends—his roommate Ranger Charles Simmons, and Hook's girlfriend, Laura—were watching television. Kevin's dog Timber, a golden retriever, and Laura's dog, Schnapps, a dachshund, also were in the room. While the temperature outside was 45 degrees, the glowing woodburning stove gave off ample amounts of heat that, according to the dial on the wall thermometer, had heated the room up to 90 degrees.

"Suddenly," Hook said, "the dogs began to act strangely. They looked at each other, panic stricken, and began to pant furiously."

The animals got up, looked around the room and moved their heads up and down, right and left, as if they were looking into every corner of the room. But there was nothing visible to the three people. They sat in place, confused by the dogs' behavior.

"Then it happened," Hook said. "The room became stone cold. I glanced at the thermometer on the wall—still 90 degrees. When we exhaled, our breath became misty, as if we were outside in frigid weather. The dogs had gone to the adjoining room and they were still panicky and barking wildly. Then, just as suddenly as it had started, the air returned to normal. We could no longer feel the icy chill or see our breath."

Hook said the dogs eventually calmed down and stopped barking. He and his friends had to coax them back into the room, but they were still anxious. But the animals weren't alone in their reaction.

"The three of us," Hook said, "sat there motionless for quite some time—dazed and confused—looking at each other and wondering what it was that we just experienced."

Haunted Campsites

Hammett mentioned that the park also has two haunted campsites—number 136 and 137—so called because they seem to be sites that demand much more attention than all of the others located throughout the park.

One day Hammett received a call to visit a family that was staying at site 137. He explained that most of these requests are of a minor nature. Oftentimes, campers may want to lodge a complaint about people at a nearby site who are being rowdy or making noise or disturbances late in the evening.

On this occasion, Hammett introduced himself to a family of four—a mother, father and two young boys, ages 4 and 6.

"I could read the parents when I arrived," Hammett said. "They were glancing at each other. It was pretty obvious that they were hesitant to talk to me."

After a little encouragement, the father explained that his youngest son was having an imaginary conversation with somebody that they couldn't see. But, he also was outside the camper when they awoke in the morning, and the boy told them "his friend" let him out.

Hammett, who could see the boy talking to no one on the other side of the nearby picnic table, suggested that the boy let himself out, or that the older son opened the door for the younger brother.

The parents said they had questioned the older brother and he denied having anything to do with it. Also, the father added, the camper door was locked from the inside—and it is unable to be locked from the outside There was no way the young boy could have gotten out and also relocked the camper, the parents stressed.

Hammett walked over to the little boy and asked him who he was talking to.

The youngster pointed across the table and said, "That man."

Hammett said he and everyone looked, but they could see nothing at all.

"I asked, 'Is he still there?' " Hammett recalled. "And the boy said, 'Yeah!' When I asked him what color the man's clothes were, the boy said he didn't know. His mother said he didn't know his colors by name, so she brought out a bunch of crayons and he began to draw the man and show me the colors with his crayons."

As he roughed out an outline of his invisible friend and began to fill in the drawing with colors that matched the Confederate uniforms of the time, the boy announced that the man was leaving. When asked, he pointed toward an area of brush and said the man was walking away in that direction.

"The drawing was definitely of a Confederate soldier," Hammett recalled. "The hat had a wide brim, made of cloth, rather than a small cap. It was a slouch hat, like most of the prisoners worn. The colors matched, too. They weren't gray, like most people expect, but more of a greenish butternut color."

I asked what the parents and Hammett said when the incident was over.

"The parents were bewildered," he replied, "and I left it at that. We just ended up scratching our heads. There wasn't any answer that could explain it."

Hammett added that the campsite where the incident with the boy occurred is the same place where a woman reported that someone with a very cold hand grabbed her ankle. But, he can offer no explanation for why this site seems to host more activity than others.

"We have campsites located on old burial sites that we don't get reports from," Hammett said. "We also have campsites in the park that are closer to the site of the Civil War smallpox hospitals, and they don't cause us as much of a problem. But we've had to move a lot of people off those two sites in particular."

On Permanent Guard Duty

Kevin Hook explained that Maryland Route 5 travels through Point Lookout State Park and ends at the main entrance to the lighthouse, or at "the point area" as the spot is called. This tip of land, surrounded on three sides by water, has an 8-foot-high, chainlink fence that encloses the lighthouse. The entire restricted area of this tip of the point is off limits to the public because it is owned by the U.S. Navy, which operates a radar tracking facility just a few yards away from the lighthouse.

One evening while Hook was patrolling the point area, he was stopped by a young couple in a Jeep Wrangler. They were heading north, away from the point and only about 100 feet from the lighthouse.

"The driver reached out his arm and flagged me down," Hook said. "I became cautious, not sure of what was wrong."

The male driver paused and Hook thought the young man seemed embarrassed to share what was on his mind. Eventually, the driver paused and said, "My girlfriend here has a question. I think it is stupid, but she wants me to ask you anyway."

Hook looked over at the woman and asked how he could help her.

She said, "I don't want you to think I am crazy, but is there someone who patrols inside the fenced area around the lighthouse?"

Hook said, "No. There is no one permitted inside the fenced area because of the tracking facility."

The girl replied, "I swear, I saw someone inside the fence, close to the lighthouse, just a few minutes ago. He was wearing a dark uniform and had a small flat hat, and was pacing back and forth. He was carrying a long rifle on his shoulder with a long knife sticking off the top of the gun."

Hook said he repeated that no one was permitted inside the fenced area, but he also realized that the young woman had accurately described a Civil War soldier on guard duty.

Smiling, Hook said he told the young woman, "You are not the first person to report seeing a possible ghost, and I'll add this to my list of stories."

In Search Of . . .

While driving north on Route 5, Ranger Hammett was half way between the causeway and the exit road from the park's campground. He said his primary attention was focused on the narrow shoulderless road to his front, but in his rearview mirror he caught a glimpse of a figure of a young man that seem to leap from the wood on the campground side of the road. Since whatever it was seemed to disappear into the woods on the Tanner's Creek Side of the pavement, Hammett immediately returned to the site of the sighting to investigate.

"My first thought was that I had observed a trespasser, fleeing the area," Hammett said, explaining that occasionally campsites are pilfered in the search for food, beer and sodas left unattended. After examining the area, he was unable to find any type of path on either side of the road, or any evidence of a human or animal crossing.

49

"The woods on both sides of the road was thick with poison ivy and green briar," Hammett recalled. "It would have been humanly impossible to successfully exit and then reenter the woods at the speed I had observed."

After analyzing the sighting and the results of his investigation, Hammett began to question what he had seen and look for other explanations.

He recalled that the sun was low in the western sky, the window of the patrol car was dusty, there were alternating shadows caused by the loblolly pines that streaked across the road and car window.

"I have often seen out of the corner of my eye," he said, "something that looks like the figure of a person. But when I look in its direction, I discover a coat on a wall hook, or light illuminating the trunk of a tree."

But, although he questioned the sighting, Hammett added that he had witnessed this young figure running across the same spot in the road on several occasions. It seems to occur during the day, just as Hammett's vehicle passes and the ranger said he always notices the figure in his rearview mirror.

"The man always crosses in the same direction," Hammett said. "I have experienced the same phenomenon while driving different vehicles at different times of the day and different times of the year. I have never gotten a good enough look at the intruder to identify him or describe his attire in detail. I can say my impression fits that of the 19th century Civil War Confederate soldier. The site of my observations is only a few feet from one of two Confederate cemeteries located at Point Lookout. The cemeteries were used to bury Confederates who died while prisoners in the Civil War prison."

Hammett said the crossing also is near the site of the Civil War smallpox hospital, where quarantined Confederate prisoners were held.

"If the man would have been making the same trek during the Civil War," Hammett said, "he would have been running in a route, taking him directly away from the smallpox hospital."

One of the many escape tactics used by Confederate prisoners was to trick their Union captors into sending the Rebels into the smallpox hospital. The prisoners, Hammett said, used hot coals to burn "pox" marks that looked like smallpox marks on their skin.

"Since there were no walls around the hospital," Hammett said, "and Union guards kept their distance from the hospital, the tactic made it easier to escape."

Hammett wonders if this recurring figure could be the spirit of a Confederate prisoner who escaped from the smallpox hospital, only to die as a result of actually contracting the contagious smallpox while faking illness in the hospital. Could the figure be a Rebel who was buried in the adjoining soggy cemetery during the Civil War?

If one believes hauntings are associated with tragic events, Hammett said the possible situations with this prisoner qualifies in several ways. Not only did he die a tragic death as a prisoner of war at Point Lookout, but he and others were buried unceremoniously in soggy graves wrapped only in a blanket or sheet.

"After death," Hammett said, "the bodies were not left to rest in peace. In 1910, the federal government returned to Point Lookout and exhumed the bodies because some body parts were eroding into Tanners Creek. Since a series of woods fires and rot had destroyed the primitive wooden markers which originally marked the soldiers' graves, the workers buried what body parts they could find in a mass grave near the Civil War monument in Scotland."

Hammett said, "It has been suggested I have observed the spirits of Confederate soldiers wandering in search of their remains where they were originally buried."

Overnight in the Fort

Hammett explained that visitors to Point Lookout State Park often claim to see Civil War soldiers wandering the grounds. However, all of these sightings are not of ghosts. Tourists and campers often see Point Lookout's volunteers, who dress in Civil War costumes for reenactments.

One unusual event occurred at Fort Lincoln, one of three earthen forts built by the Union Army to defend the prison from an attack by Confederate forces. Fort Lincoln is the only defense structure that remained when the state of Maryland purchased the area in the 1960s. The fort's internal buildings behind the dirt mounds have been reconstructed by volunteers with an interest in the Civil War.

51

Many believe the site of this restored fort is haunted.

On a cold February evening, one of the park volunteer Civil War soldiers was preparing to spend the night in the restored Fort Lincoln guardhouse.

Hammett said that several volunteers had arranged to spend the night together, so they would be able to be on the scene early and be prepared for events that were planned at the fort the next day. But, the rest of the group that was supposed to arrive on Friday night never showed up.

"The brave soldier," Hammett said, "decided to spend the night in the fort anyway."

While he was outside, gathering an armload of firewood to carry back inside the guardhouse, the soldier stooped down in front of the guardhouse when he said he heard a bullet flutter overhead. He then said he heard the glass in the guardhouse window shatter and fall to the ground a few feet away, and at the same instant the lens to a kerosene lantern hanging from one of the corner posts supporting the interior bunks cracked.

"Needless to say," Hammett said, "the volunteer soldier did not stay in the fort that night. I found the volunteer reenactor the following morning camping in his pickup camper. We returned to Fort Lincoln to inspect the damage. The window was not broken."

Summary

Those who visit Point Lookout are impressed by its solitude. Standing on the southern tip of Maryland's Western Shore, one can see only water as far as the horizon to the south and east. In the distance to the west, about five miles away, are treetops indicating the coastline of the Commonwealth of Virginia. Especially at night, or during early morning at Point Lookout, when you are completely alone, you can imagine what it must be like to stand on the edge of the earth.

At that moment, forcing the mind to travel back nearly 140 years, one can only envision how the tens of thousands of Confederate prisoners and hundreds of sick Union troops survived cold winters beside the water and lasted through the hot lower peninsula summers with hordes of hungry mosquitoes and thick waves of high humidity.

Hammett said he once told his interpreters there is no need for them to make up ghost stories about the park, enough real suffering and agony have occurred there. At Point Lookout, infected limbs were amputated in wretched fashion, worn out bodies were buried in soggy graves, boisterous prisoners were shot in their tents and desperate escapees actually drowned off shore.

Many believe that some victims of sudden death refuse, or are unable to, give up their spirits and pass to the other side. If so, Point Lookout and Point Lookout Lighthouse—along with other surviving isolated lighthouses and Civil War forts around the country—may be the place to look out for them.

Historical notes: Located at the southern-most tip of Maryland's Western Shore, Point Lookout was known as a popular summer resort— with a hotel. approximately 100 beach cottages, a wharf and lighthouse (built in the 1830s)—when the Civil War began.

In 1862, the U.S. government established an Army hospital for Northern solders at the site. Early in 1863, a small number of Confederate prisoners were placed there. Most of these captives were citizens of Southern Maryland who were sympathetic to the Confederate cause.

After the Battle of Gettysburg, construction began at the camp on facilities capable of holding 10,000 prisoners of war. Over the course of the War of Northern Aggression, as the Civil War was called in the South, records indicate 52,264 individuals were imprisoned at Point Lookout and approximately 3,500 died.

Point Lookout was used primarily for enlisted men. Most officers were sent to Fort Delaware. Both prison camps also held political prisoners—primarily individuals who were identified to be critical of the Union. One of Point Lookout's better known prisoners was Sidney Lanier, a writer, poet, professor of literature and musician.

Point Lookout Prison Camp for Confederates by the late Edwin W. Beitzell, and published by the St. Mary's County Historical Society—P.O. Box 212, Leonardtown, MD 20650—is a fascinating history of the region and its citizens, plus the prison camp and its prisoners and captors. The book includes diary entries, photographs, drawings and details on the harsh conditions and daily life at Point Lookout. The book also is valuable since it provides a view of the Civil War and the life of Confederate prisoners from the perspective of those who fought against the Union. Unfortunately, with increasing misguided emphasis on *political correctness—*

which seems to be antagonistic toward any efforts to understand or support certain aspects of the Southern Cause, including states' rights against a growing federal bureaucratic monster—such books will become increasingly more difficult to locate.

Features: Today, Point Lookout State Park, operated by the state of Maryland Forest & Park Service since 1965, includes 1,046 acres. Three forts were erected to protect the "nation's largest Civil War prison." Some of the earthen mounds of Fort Lincoln still remain. Today, visitors can walk through the barracks, outbuildings and see the earthen battlements. This restored fortification's buildings and barracks were reconstructed by volunteers and reenactors from the 20th Maine. There are two impressive monuments that stand in memory of the prisoners who died at Point Lookout. The first was built by the state of Maryland in 1876, and the second was erected by the U.S. government in the early 1900s.

There are a large number of recreational opportunities at Point Lookout State Park, including camping, boating, boat rentals, hiking, fishing, crabbing and swimming.

During Halloween season, there are special haunted events and tours that attract thousands. Also, during the afternoon on the first Saturday in November, Point Lookout Lighthouse is open to the public for a few hours. Hundreds of visitors have lined up hoping to gain an opportunity to walk through the historic haunted building. If you are interested in touring the lighthouse, arrive early. According to park officials, hundreds of people have been turned away in recent years because of the large turnout and the limited amount of time that the building is open to the public.

Sightings: Point Lookout Lighthouse, the shoreline, certain cottages, old roads through the park and campsites Number 136 and 137.

Contact: Point Lookout State Park, Post Office Box 48, Scotland, MD 20687. Phone: (301) 872-5688 (office); (888) 432-2267 (camp reservations).

John Bullen House
c. 1775

Delaware Made's 'Welcoming Ghost'

In the center of Dover, Delaware, the John Bullen House at 214 South State Street offers visitors a glimpse of the fine work of its original 18th-century builder and owner. The well known master carpenter constructed his home in 1775, and it has seen the comings and goings of First State history for 225 years.

Venture inside this historic building and you will hear shopkeeper Tom Smith's stories about Bullen's excellent craftsmanship, but he will also speak of the fine skills of today's 21st century Delaware artisans. You see, Smith is the proprietor of "Delaware Made General Store," which now occupies Bullen's former home, and Smith takes pride in offering jewelry, art, apparel, candles, artist prints, books, copperware, souvenirs and just about anything related to or made in the Diamond State.

If you can, linger a bit after your purchase is tucked safely into its bag. And if the shop's pace allows you and Tom a little time to engage in conversation, there's a good chance you will hear quite a bit more about the house that Bullen built—including the

strong possibility that old departed John's spirit may still be floating around the premises.

It was 11 years ago, in 1989, when Tom and his partner
Schuyler Anderson, were working on the floor in the old dining
room, which is located to the right of the present entry hall.

It was well past 11 o'clock, very late and dark, when the two
men heard someone whistling. It sounded like it was coming from
beyond the closed door that led to the entry hall.

Tom said he got up, went out into the hall and there was no
one there. He also opened the front door and looked up and
down State Street. Still, there was no one is sight.

"I came back in and was surprised," Tom said, recalling his
reaction to his first and only encounter with the spirit. "I just
couldn't figure it out. There was no one around, and the sound
was very loud. It wasn't a recognizable tune."

Tom said the two men decided that it was "just one of those
things, probably the people upstairs." But, a short time later, Tom
asked the couple in the second-floor apartment if they had come
in whistling late on that particular night."

Their reaction, Tom said, was interesting.

"They laughed," Tom remembered, "and then the wife told me,
'No! It was probably the ghost!' "

Then they shared their strange occurrence.

Late one evening, the woman said to Tom, she and her husband heard someone come into the downstairs hall, through the
locked door. Then they heard footsteps come up the stairs to the
second floor and head all the way up to the attic.

"She said her husband got up, looked around, saw nothing
and went up to check the attic," Tom recalled. "There was no one
there. That was their only occurrence, and it was shortly after they
moved in. So, my partner and I decided that if nothing had happened to them, and nothing happened to us, it must be a friendly
ghost. And that was the only time we heard anything."

But, just about two years ago, when a new person moved into
the upstairs apartment, the ghost apparently resurfaced.

"Again, as in our case and with the other tenant," Tom said, "it
was late at night, about 11:30, and the new people heard someone open the downstairs door. Then they heard footsteps walking
up the stairway to the second floor, but this time they went back
down and out the front door. The woman told me she was kind of

frightened, because she knew the door was locked, and no one could get in."

Soon after that happened, the woman noticed a strange event in her bedroom.

"Across the wall, just above her bed," Tom said, "she had three pictures arranged side by side. One day she came into that room and one of the end pictures was off the wall and lying in the center of her bed. But it was physically impossible for that to happen. If it fell off the wall, it would have landed on the floor below the hook. She said it was as if someone took the picture down and placed it in the center of the bed."

Tom said the woman put the picture back on the wall and a few days later it was on the bed again.

"Then she told me," Tom said, " ' Well maybe this ghost doesn't like how I have arranged the pictures.' So she rearranged them in a different order and they haven't moved since. She said since the events occurred soon after she moved in, the tenant said she named the ghost The Welcoming Ghost."

Laughing, Tom added that the title makes perfect sense, because all three groups of people who have had any experience with the spirit say it occurred when they were new to the Bullen home, and major unexplained events never occurred to them again.

Looking around at the historic home that is more than two centuries old, Tom spoke with respect about the builder's skills. The present merchant also treats the building with the reverence which he said it deserves.

"This is a wonderful building," Tom said. "Much of the original woodwork is still here, in the same places that John Bullen placed it in the 18th century. Unfortunately, sometimes I must put nail holes in the walls or push a pin into the woodwork, I say, 'Excuse me, John Bullen. I'm sorry, but I have to do this.'

"But this is a great old house. We were fortunate that it was available when we were looking for a place to open the shop. As for John Bullen, I think he's a nice ghost, otherwise he might do things that might scare me off. But as long as I don't do anything to wreck his house, I'm sure everything will be just fine."

Attractions: Publishes *The General Store Gazette* several times a year, informing shoppers about the wide variety of Delaware oriented items. In addition, it provides details on special events, sales, holiday hours and, the best part, an essay by Tom about the area and its people. The 1999 Winter issue included a delightful Christmas story. Also, books by Myst and Lace Publishers are available at this shop.

Tours: Offers spring, summer and fall walking tours of the the central Dover area on Saturdays, as well as a special Ghost Tour on Halloween.

Activity: In the downstairs entry hall and stairway. Upstairs in one of the apartments (no public access).

Contact: Delaware Made General Store, (originally the John Bullen House, built in 1775), 214 South State Street, Dover, Del. 19901; telephone (302) 736-1419.

Cellar Gourmet

A Dining Delight in Historic New Castle

Old Fashioned Goodness with a Healthy Touch

Jane at the Cellar Gourmet

H er name is Jane, at least that's what they call her. To be honest, no one can be sure of what her identity really is. But a regular customer suggested the name and it sort of stuck, so Jane it is.

Jane resides in New Castle, Delaware, and, from time to time, she appears. When she does materialize, it's only in the kitchen of the Cellar Gourmet, a basement eatery at 208 Delaware Street, right in the center of the historic district directly across the street from the court house.

Sue and Kristina, her daughter, operate the restaurant business, which is open for breakfast and lunches and includes an ice cream parlor and catering service. According to the history of the building presented on the back of the menu, the historic building in the center of town was built about 1802 and is also known as the William B. Janvier House.

A very interesting piece of the structure's architecture is the old well that can be seen beside the stone fireplace in the Cellar Gourmet dining room. The well's walls travel between the Janvier House, that hosts the Cellar Gourmet restaurant and its first-floor gift shop, and the adjacent Gilpin House, the present site of the Wilmington Trust Company branch office.

Sue and Kristina have been associated with the Cellar Gourmet for more than five years and owners of the operation for the last 18 months.

"The former owner told us she saw a figure of a woman in the kitchen," Kristina said. "I was working there that day, but I didn't see anything. But the descriptions are always the same. They say she has shoulder length brown hair and that she appears in the kitchen."

Although the sightings are irregular, they still continue to occur. A woman saw the ghostly lady about a year ago, and a man who was in the restaurant saw the apparition in the kitchen only six months ago, Kristina said.

When Jane the Ghost isn't making an appearance, she still makes sure her invisible presence is noticed.

On one occasion, a cookie jar lid flew off its base and fell to the floor as Kristina was walking from the dining room into the front counter room area. Another time, when an employee and her husband were arguing in the front room, a replacement lid flew from the top of the cookie jar and smashed at the couple's feet. No one was nearby, and there was no logical reason for the ceramic object to have taken flight.

"They stopped arguing," Kristina said, "so I guess the activity served its purpose."

Action also occurs near the well, located in a shadowy corner beside the large attractive stone fireplace. A piece of thick glass allows customers to peer down into the centuries old well, and Sue said if you stand at the top opening, in the bank next door, you can look straight down into the well.

Kristina said there is a table beside the well where workers usually sit when they have a chance to take a break.

"I've been there," Kristina added, "and I've felt something nearby or felt a hand touch my shoulder softly. It's not a hard touch. It's very soft but noticeable. I've also felt something or someone touching my hair, but there's never anyone around. I just brush it off and keep moving."

When Sue arrived alone, as she usually does each morning, she heard voices talking in the dining room. It bothered her so much that she called Kristina at home and told her to come to the restaurant.

"When I arrived, there was nothing to be heard," Kristina said. "My mom said it was happening before she opened the shop, while she was getting things ready for the day. It sounded like it does if you're in another room and you can hear people talking, but you can't understand their words, can't make them out."

The incidents are not constant. They happen in spurts. Sometime there will be a long period of inactivity, then one or two small thing will occur, just to let you know the ghost is still around.

"During the year and a half that we've been here," she said, "I've seen dishes fly off the shelves. I've had glasses fall and not break. Other times, items have fallen but landed across the room, instead of below the shelf where they were standing. But things seem to happen most when there's negative activity, like arguments or loud noise or when there's a lot going on when it gets busy and wild in here."

Having a resident spirit can be an asset, Kristina said.

"It's not something we advertise," she said, "but when people ask, or when some people come in and say they feel there's something here, we talk to them about what has happened over the years. This town and the building are historic and they have been here for a long time. This house was used as a saloon, a private home. Travelers stopped here for centuries, so many people have passed through these doors. I think it's kind of neat to have something here. We wonder what or who it might be, but it would be impossible to figure out the identity of our spirit even though I'd like to know more about who it is."

In Kristina's opinion, the strangest series of events happened on Christmas Eve 1998. As new owners, she and her mother had decided to remain open only half of the day. Since so many people would be out shopping, it didn't make sense to follow the normal schedule.

As Sue usually does, she arrived early in the morning to prepare the food and soups. She was alone in the restaurant during the earliest part of the day. Everything was fine until later in the morning, after her help had arrived.

"An employee and I were working at the front counter," Kristina said, "when my mom came out of the kitchen and said the stove had been damaged. When we looked, the glass top of the stove was shattered. It was as if someone had taken a fist and hit it real hard, and there was no explanation.

"Then, only about five minutes later," Kristina continued, "I heard the cabinet doors up front slam shut very hard and loudly. I went up to look for the cause of the disturbance, but no one was there. I remember standing there, looking at one cabinet, and suddenly the one next to it was doing the same thing. There are four doors, and all of them opened and slammed shut on their own. I remember thinking, 'I'm really not liking this right now.' "

That day was the worst of all, Kristina said. But the series of bizarre Christmas Eve incidents hadn't ended. As they were preparing to leave and shut things up for the day, Kristina said there was heavy knocking at the front door, on the first-floor, street-level entrance.

"I ran up and down the stairs at least four times to answer whatever it was that was banging on the door, trying to get in," Kristina said. "Again, there was no one in sight. That was a little frightening, and that was one of the worst days." Laughing, Kristina added, "We weren't open this past year, in 1999, on Christmas Eve. Our official reason was it wasn't that busy the previous year. So if anything happened we weren't there to hear it."

Sightings: The ghost has been seen in the back kitchen. Other incidents have occurred in the dining room, in the front ice cream parlor area and at the front, street-level door.

Attractions: Located in the heart of historic New Castle, Delaware. A gift shop is on the first floor. Among its items are Myst and Lace Publishers books. There is an ice cream parlor on the cellar level, along with the restaurant. The restaurant and catering service are available for special events.

Contact: Cellar Gourmet, 208 Delaware Street, New Castle, DE 19720; telephone (302) 323-0999.

We're Not Ghostbusters

E ach Halloween, ghosts command center stage. Old horror flicks about unsettled graveyard spirits boost movie rental sales. A white bedsheet, with a few strategically placed holes, passes off as the perfect, economical party disguise. And age-old folktales of the unexplained are whispered over the flickering lights of sour-faced jack o'lanterns.

But for ghost hunters around the country, All Hallows Eve is just another day, no different than any other, for their quest to capture evidence of life beyond the grave is a year-round search that is not dictated by passing seasons or holiday hoopla.

It was early in the fall, more than 10 years ago—before the current high-tech days of digital photography and voice activated tape recorders—when I met with two men at a small village located near New Jersey's haunted Pine Barrens, home of the famous Jersey Devil.

Zebulon, who went by the name of Zeb, was a middle school science teacher. His cousin, Marty, was a contractor. Since their days together in elementary school, they spent their spare time reading and talking about the Bermuda Triangle, UFO sightings, ghosts, local legends and life after death.

During our conversation in a small cottage they owned in a remote wooded area of the Garden State, they recalled how in the mid-1980s they decided to do something they thought no one

63

else had ever done—track down and prove that ghosts exist using a tape recorder and the earliest, oversized models of video cameras.

They knew ghosts had fascinated people for centuries. But, at the same time, the search to prove the existence of another dimension or un-Earthly creatures had frustrated those who had conducted similar searches. Despite others' failures, the two men decided to give it a try.

Thrill of the Hunt

"This wasn't the case of one or two people coming forward and saying they had seen something," Zeb said. "There have been thousands of people who claim they've seen a ghost or a figure or some form of energy. We believed there was something to it, that they were telling the truth. We said there has to be something out there. We decided to try to capture a voice on a cassette tape, or an apparition or sighting on a videotape."

"Also," Marty added, "for every person who was willing to speak up and say he saw something, there were a hundred more who were afraid to talk. They don't want to be laughed at. So we figured we were just hearing from those sitting at the tip of the iceberg. We knew there was a lot of stories offering tons of potential."

After putting up posters at several convenience stores, craft fairs and public bulletin boards in supermarkets, Zeb got a call from a woman who wanted them to come and investigate a sighting outside her house.

"She lived in a standard, middle class development on land that used to be a farm," Marty recalled. "She was very nice, and we went over to talk to her one night after work, to lay out the ground rules and hear her story."

The sighting was not what the ghost-hunting duo had expected. The woman complained that a phantom dog—not a human-like apparition—was prowling around her yard at night, scratching on the back door and even leaving marks. But each time she reached the outside entrance and turned on the patio light, the scratching stopped. When she looked outside the window, there was nothing to see.

"But," Zeb said, "she told us she also had seen this strange dog, with a misty shape, roaming in her backyard in the middle of the night. She didn't own a dog, and neither did her neighbors on either side. When she went outside to follow the animal, it was gone. No footprints, nothing. That freaked her out. She also said one neighbor, who had stayed over one night, saw it too. But they could never catch it or get a picture."

The ghost hunters and the homeowner reached an agreement. Zeb and Marty would set up their equipment and spend three nights camped out in the woman's backyard. They selected a weekend and were there from Friday night until Monday morning. After positioning three video cameras, operated by hand-held, remote control boxes, and two tape records, each man took up a comfortable position in an oversized sleeping bag and waited.

They took shifts sleeping, and both Zeb and Marty had a new 35 mm camera loaded with high speed film. On that weekend, and during another about a month later, they neither witnessed nor recorded any unusual activity.

"In the end, the woman was thrilled," Zeb said, shaking his head sadly. "She told me that right after our initial visit to discuss the overall plan, all the activity stopped. While that was good for her, it didn't help us any. It wasn't what we were trying to do."

"Right!" added Marty. "We're not trying to drive them off, the spirits or ghosts or whatever they are. We want to get them on film, as evidence. It doesn't do us any good to have nothing there to film or record. We're not ghostbusters, we're ghost hunters. There's a very big difference."

On their next three investigations, which involved overnights at a restaurant, school and private residence, the same thing happened. By the time they arrived for their overnight investigation, the spirits had apparently moved on.

"This was getting very frustrating," Zeb said. "So we decided that on the next trip we would meet the person at a restaurant first, not in the home or haunted site, and then just show up according to our agreement. That way, the ghost wouldn't be able to hear us talking and making plans and would end up being surprised."

The ghost wasn't the only one that was amazed at the results.

The next strange encounter took place at an antique shop, filled with shelves of old books, dolls, toys, jewelry, records and furniture. There were thousands of objects in the shop, according to Marty, who said neither he nor Zeb had ever been there until they arrived at 10 p.m. one Saturday evening with a key provided by the storekeeper. All of the arrangements had been made over the telephone, during a call from the owner's private residence, so the ghost was literally in the dark.

"It was ice cold in the place," Zeb said, "even though it was August and there was no air conditioning and the building had been locked up tight. You would think it would have been hot as an oven, but the minute we walked into that door, it was like entering an ice house . . . ."

"Or a morgue," Marty added, smiling. "I tell you, it was very eerie, extremely strange and pretty darn scary."

The men set up their equipment and aimed two cameras at a display case where the owner had indicated that much of the strange activity occurred during the nights.

Try to Remain Calm

"He told us when he opened the shop in the mornings," Marty said, "that his stuff was on the floor. When we said it could just be vibrations or items falling off the counter, or even rodents moving about, he laughed and said the objects had been locked in the counter cases and there was no way they could get out. Plus, the cases were still locked when he came in, but the jewelry was on the floor. That was a new one for us, very exciting to be honest, and we told him we were eager to stay the night."

Zeb laughed, and added, "Yeah! He gave us the key and said, 'You two have to be crazy. I rush out of there as soon as it starts to get dark. Good luck!' I'll admit, that made me a little frightened, but this was the first place that we were able to enter that had such high potential, so we agreed."

"What could we do?" snapped Marty. "We were claiming to be ghost hunters. Were we going to say, 'No. We can't go in there. It sounds too scary.' People would look at us like we were really nuts then. I mean, first they think we're crazy for doing this in the first place. But then they would really think we had a few bolts loose if we said we were ghost hunting but turned down the places with the best potential, that had the most active ghosts."

Acknowledging that I had a very good understanding of their dilemma, I urged them to continue. Again, unfortunately, there was little success that evening. As soon as they turned on their video equipment, the cold left the room and so did the ghost.

"It was as if the thing knew what we were after and wasn't going to let us have even a tiny morsel of success," Marty said, still annoyed as he recalled the incident. "I got that feeling the moment the ice cold air disappeared. It was like something sucked it away. But we stuck it out, through the whole long boring night, sleeping in shifts in those uncomfortable antique chairs. But, again, no luck."

They returned to Zeb's home, where they stored their equipment, packed it away in his hall closet and headed for work.

During the next week, Zeb said he began to notice small changes inside his house. Furniture was moved, not a lot but slightly. Small items—like his car keys and coffee cups and silverware and knickknacks—were missing or out of place.

"I would put something down," Zeb said, "and then a few minutes later it would be gone. Like my glasses case. I would usually just come home, drop it on my desk, walk away. But I would come back 10 minutes later and it was missing. Then I'd look through my pockets, in the kitchen, anywhere else I might usually leave it, and not find it. But, the next time I passed by my desk, the case with my glasses in it was back where it should be.

"At first I thought I was going nuts. I mean it. It's the kind of thing you don't notice right away, then after the fourth or fifth time in a week or two, you say, 'Hey! Something is strange here.' The same thing was happening with my car keys. But that would really get me upset. I've got an extra set of glasses, but my key chain has my house key, storage shed key, other keys. If I lose them, I can't start the car and will be late for work. One day they were gone for about an hour."

Pausing, Zeb said he was really angry. He was rushing around and began screaming and yelling through the whole house. Finally, he said in frustration, he let all his anger out.

"By then I knew it was a ghost, probably the one that had followed us back in the equipment from the antique shop. I told Marty at the time, but he said I was nuts. He laughed at me about it, would tease me. On this day when I was really late, I shouted out, 'Listen, you damn ghost or whatever the hell you are, I've had it! I need those damn keys right now! I'm going to go into my bedroom and wait five minutes. When I come back, I want them on the kitchen table. And they better be there!' "

Zeb admitted he had no idea what he was going to do if the keys weren't returned. But at the time screaming at the phantom seemed like a good idea and it made him feel much better.

67

Casually, he passed me a black, old-fashioned earring. It was not pierced, had a screw-like attachment that you had to twist to affix to the earlobe.

"When I came back into the kitchen," Zeb said, " that earring was sitting on the table. My keys were on a nearby chair. I know they weren't on that chair before, and I know that earring wasn't anywhere in the house. I don't have a wife or girlfriend. I think it came from the antique shop with the ghost. I think that was signal that it was sorry, and I firmly believe that it left after that con- frontation, because that was the end of all of the strange activity in my place."

After that story we discussed the benefit of talking to ghosts. Both Zeb and Marty said they believe very strongly that doing so can solve a majority of problems.

There's Something Right Here

"You can't live in a state of denial," Marty said. "The UFO people say 'There's something out there.' We say 'There's some- thing right here,' with us right now. We just can't see it or touch it, but it's around. I believe it. I have no doubts."

According to Zeb, these restless souls are probably seeking attention. "They need someone to tell them what to do, to give them a reason to move on, to tell them it's all right to go. And sometimes we have to yell at them for messing up our human lives. I tell them that they had their chance, that they have no right to come back and steal my keys and make me late for work. If they want to be quiet and live in the closet and not interfere with what I have to do, it's fine. But, eventually, they are better off heading to the other side, moving on to be with their relatives and friends."

During the years that they have conducted investigations, Zeb and Marty said their clients have included small businessmen, corporate executives, educators, homeowners, owners of historic sites and even managers of cemeteries.

"We spend a lot of time in graveyards," Marty said, smiling. "But those visits aren't usually productive. Plus, it's cold and mis- erable to be out there all night long. Outside sounds and back- ground noise, plus nearby artificial light, tend to interfere with what our equipment is trying to record. It's not that I'm afraid out there, among the tombstones, it's just not very productive."

Zeb stressed that hauntings are not limited to historic build-ings or vacant mansions that look like they were built specifically for a horror movie. Contemporary homes, new strip malls, gas sta-tions and even beach houses have offered stories of unexplained incidents. But people like Zeb and Marty are not interested in the story, their main goal is to capture a ghostly figure in action—on a video film on in a still photograph—or to record a spectral sound on an audio cassette.

While the legends and folktales and more recent stories of events at the site may cause them to arrive upon the scene, catch-ing the evidence is their sole and ultimate goal. If and when that occurs they said they intend to share it with agencies and aca-demic research centers that focus on parapsychology.

"There are these surveys, published every October in all kinds of magazines, from *Women's Day* to *Playboy*," Zeb said. "Some of them say that close to 40 percent of people believe in ghosts. But I think it's more than that. Now, if you ask how many people like to read or hear about ghost stories, it's probably more like 90 percent. Tell people a good ghost story and they're all ears. Tell them you're into hunting ghosts and all of them will listen, but a good number of them will walk off and think you're nuts. But, so what? I'm having fun."

Investigative Techniques

Most people are unaware that good ghost hunting involves a lot of long-range work and planning.

For most investigations, Zeb and Marty explained:

> • An initial meeting occurs, usually at the business person's or homeowner's site. Investigators usually trav-el in pairs, for both safety and authentication purposes. During this first site visit, they evaluate the situation, assess the validity of the case and attempt to rule out the possibility of a hoax.
> • They conduct library and courthouse research of land records and news articles to review the history of the structure and surrounding area, looking at previous owners and trying to see if any tragedies—such as mur-ders or suicides—may have happened there.

- There is a review of blueprints or diagrams of the home to determine the rooms or areas with the most activity. This also helps them decide upon the sites where cameras and audio equipment will be positioned during the on-site investigation.
- There is a two-hour set-up and take-down process. Since most investigations occur overnight, homeowners must decide if they will or will not be present and what their role will be during the lengthy research exercise.

Zeb and Marty said they sometimes will bring along additional personnel to help man cameras and perform other chores during overnight investigations. Since they are located in different parts of a home, personnel maintain contact by using walkie-talkies.

While they have not yet recorded an apparition—or figure— during any of their site visits, both men have said they have felt the presence of something other than Earthly beings. Dramatic changes in temperature, footsteps, slamming doors, whistling, moaning and being touched and pushed by an unseen force have occurred. Unfortunately, none of these incidents have yielded photographic evidence.

"Once, just as a videotape ran out," Marty said, "an unopened door flew open, but I was changing the tape at the time. It's almost as if the ghosts can see what we are doing and they begin to act up when we are unable to capture them. They aren't stupid. They know what we're after. I think they enjoy making it a game."

"Sure, they know what we're trying to do," Marty agreed. "But we'll get them. As technology advances, we'll get better equipment that will be voice or motion activated. When that happens, we won't be busy changing tapes and having to stare in the darkness all night. We'll make informed decisions on which sites to visit and when, and the cameras will do most of the work for us.

"They've got them now, but they're very expensive. When they come down in price, we'll get them and be better armed, equipment wise, when we go into a haunted house."

Both men said a major benefit of their investigations is the peace of mind they provide to those who have seen strange things, have lived in fear or who have been frustrated.

"They are happy to see us, to talk to us," Marty said. "Most of these people are afraid to talk about what they are going through to anyone but their most trusted friend or relatives. They are very afraid that if they share what is going on in their home, people will think they are crazy and actually laugh at them. Also, there's the age-old haunted house factor."

What's that? I wondered.

Marty continued, "Remember when you were a kid, growing up, and there was that old, run down farmhouse or mansion on the edge of town with a big woods around it? On Friday nights, for fun, a bunch of kids would go out there and spy to see if they could spot any ghosts. Later, when they got older and braver—or nastier—the same kids would sneak up and bang on the doors or throw rocks at the old place and run away. Well, there are a lot of people who don't want anyone to know they live in the town's haunted house. They just want it fixed, they want it calm again. But they need to share their experiences with someone. So the only understanding people they can find are ghost hunters like us."

"We make them feel real good," Zeb said, nodding, "especially when we can tell them that they aren't the only ones who are having these types of problems. But we're very clear that we cannot make the ghosts go away. Even though that happens sometimes, it's only by accident. We don't say prayers. We don't light candles or burn incense. We don't claim to cleanse or harmonize or exorcise any evil spirits. We only go in there to get the facts. We're trying to capture a sighting. If other things work out for the owners, that's an extra benefit and good for them. Like Marty said, and like we tell them up front, we're not ghostbusters."

The other problem is that people who live in a haunted site begin to think they are imagining things. Often, they begin to question their own senses.

"We've been through that ourselves," Zeb said. "When we tell them that there are others with the same problems, they are relieved and feel better about their physical and mental states. One woman was actually crying in front of us, and they were tears of joy. She told us she was going out of her mind. The ghosts were driving her crazy. Even though we helped her feel better about herself the day of our visit, she moved before we could go back and conduct our investigation."

Shaking his head, Marty mentioned that he was quite upset when the woman sold the house, because that site offered such tremendous potential.

71

There is no charge to conduct a visit, Zeb said. But in some cases satisfied homeowners have given them a donation, which they use to buy new equipment and pay for travel expenses. One inn gave them an overnight stay and breakfast.

While their avocation may be interesting, satisfying and fun, the two men agreed there is an element of danger lurking when they approach the unknown.

Taking One Home

When asked to describe their most unsettling experiences, the ghost hunters took a few minutes to sort out their best stories from among many uncomfortable incidents they had encountered during several years' of uneventful overnight investigations.

"For me," Marty said, "it was the ghost that followed me home. It was different than the one that Zeb told you about, the one that came back in the equipment from the antique shop. In this case, we spent the night at an old seashore mansion, near Cape May. It was owned by a rum runner during Prohibition and he had secret passages all over the place. We were really excited, but it was a bust. I mean it gave us nothing. The next morning, we loaded up the two cars and headed north for home. For the two weeks after that investigation, I kept finding sand in my car. It showed up in a small pile on the front passenger seat."

Marty said he could understand that there might be some beach sand in his car for the few days after they returned, even though no one else had sat in his car. But even though he cleaned out the inside of the vehicle several times, a small pile of sand kept appearing.

"I actually believe the ghost left with me, sat in my car and left that house," Marty said. "I know you think it sounds bizarre, and I admit it does, too, but I've come up with no other explanation. The people called and told us they've had no more trouble since we came and went. This story isn't a horrifying tale, but it is bothersome, especially since I don't know where the ghost went or where it is now."

The first part of Zeb's story had to do with the screams of a small child. He pulled a small cassette tape, with a white label bearing a name and date, out of a box. After he shoved it into his recorder/player we waited a few moments, listening to a heavy hiss that made it impossible for me to distinguish any worthwhile sound.

Suddenly, Zeb pointed to the tape and shouted at the same time, "There is it! Hear it?"

Hear what? I asked.

Patiently, as if he was asked to performed the same procedure every time he had tried to show off his audio find, he hit the "rewind" button and pressed "play." Again the scratchy "hiss" escaped from the small black box.

Alerting us to get ready, Zeb held his finger in the air and, at the precise moment, pointed to the machine.

"Hear it?"

Again, I offered a puzzled look.

Over the years I've found that Zeb, Marty and other ghost hunters get very excited when they believe they have finally captured the slightest shred of what they believe to be "evidence" of the abnormal. Being on the other side of the fence, I focus on capturing what I consider *good* stories. It's a lot more interesting, more satisfying and, frankly, they are much easier to find and record.

In a way, I feel a bit sorry for the high-tech hunters, especially when most of their "captured" audio evidence sounds like a radio out of tune until they tell you, "It's saying '*Help me!*' "or "she's calling out '*Michelle!*' Can't you understand it?"

This instance was the same.

Zeb announced that what we were hearing through the annoying hiss was the voice of a young girl, who had been invisible on the grounds of a dark cemetery, calling out "Danger!"

To be polite, I nodded that I could hear it. But my weak response was generated more from politeness rather than from a firm statement of truth.

Fortunately, the rest of Zeb's story was better.

While spending an overnight in a Revolutionary War-era, country church graveyard, Zeb said he had been awakened by a voice calling out. Not waking anyone else, he grabbed his battery powered tape recorder and flashlight and headed off in search of the source of the sound. After a half-hour of tripping over low tombstones and racing through brambles, he returned to the campsite. When he checked his tape, he said he "was fortunate to capture six distinguishable instances of a voice calling."

73

He had played the best one for me.

Thanking him, I wanted to suggest that if this was his best evidence he might want to keep it to himself, for such a weak example would not support his cause. But he continued.

"The strange thing is that for some time afterwards, and not every night," Zeb said, "I would hear that girl's voice calling out at night when I was asleep. The sound would come in a soft voice, 'Danger! Danger!' She would repeat it two or three times. At first, I was annoyed. One night, when I couldn't get any sleep, I went downstairs just to walk around, and I sat in my living room on the sofa.

"Then I looked at the electric space heater, that I had left on for my pets. I have three exotic birds, and I like to keep the room warm for them in winter. The edge of the sheer curtains was laying on the top of the heater. As I looked at it the edge began to flame. I jumped up, ripped it down from the rod and put it out."

Zeb said the curtain must have been sitting on the heater for a few hours, and it could have caused the whole room to catch on fire. The smoke alone would have killed the birds.

"Was it just a coincidence?" Zeb asked. "I know the tape isn't that impressive, not to anyone who doesn't do this a lot. But the warning, the calling out to me in the dream. I believe it's all connected. For some reason, that girl was sent to help me. She stopped a tragedy from happening. So to me that's the most unusual incident I've had connected with all of this."

Author's note: In the years since my interview with Zeb and Marty I've lost touch with them, but I have met a number of other ghost hunters. Those who investigate the unusual today use the most advanced versions of video and digital cameras. They also employ voice activated digital recorders in their quest to capture evidence of the unexplained. Their exploits will be featured in future books.

Talbot County Ghost Tales

E ach of Delmarva's 14 counties is rich in history, ghost stories and legends, and Talbot County—home of such well known tourists destinations as Easton, St. Michaels, Oxford and Tilghman Island—is no exception.

Behind the shutters of historic homes on narrow side streets, below the white fog and marsh gas that seeps along the guts and necks and amidst the thick brush and groves on the peninsula flatlands, some still claim to see apparitions, specters, phantoms and witches. Even as we enter the 21st century, creepy creatures of the night remain an important part of the folklore and oral history of the Eastern Shore.

For years, I had heard from a number of people throughout Delmarva about a pair of ghost tales associated with Easton's old White Marsh Episcopal Church graveyard, located off Route 50 south of the historic town.

After presenting a storytelling program on Delmarva legends and folklore at the Historical Society of Talbot County, I casually mentioned my interest in finding the county's haunted graveyard and asked for directions. Immediately, two persons responded by saying, "You mean the 'Hole in the Wall?' "

I didn't know what they meant by that term. But I took down their directions and was told that when I reached the old cemetery, I would understand why the site was called "Hole in the Wall."

As I began to travel south on Route 50, I set my odometer at "zero" at the intersection where Maryland Route 322 turns off toward Easton and St. Michaels. Then, proceeding exactly seven miles south on Route 50—past shopping centers, the fast food district, car dealerships and the State Police Barrack (which is on the left side of the main highway)—I saw "Hole in the Wall." It was to my left, beside the northbound lane, at the top of a small hill.

Turning left on Manadier Lane, I parked on the gravel shoulder and looked up at the jagged, single-walled remnant of White Marsh Episcopal Church. The gray-and-black Maryland historical marker states that the house of worship was built originally in 1690, but the church burned in 1892. A portion—I assume the small one-wall section of the structure that stands today—was what was "partially restored" in 1977.

I took the narrow brick pathway that led up to the rounded opening where a door probably hung centuries ago. This was the original entrance to the long-gone church. An uneven, irregular portion of the front wall of the building (supported slightly with very scant portions of side walls at either corner) is all that remains today.

Walking through the open arched entrance, I stepped upon the brick floor and noticed the bronze plaque with the name of one of the earliest pastors and his wife. The marker was set into a rectangular brick outline that reminded me very much of a grave.

With no walls, it's easy to view the worn headstones that indicate old, and more recent, gravesites scattered on three sides of the church foundation. It's a small, country-type resting place, not jammed with rows and rows of markers and statues that you tend to find in city and suburban cemeteries. Thankfully, big business and modern-day progress seem to have left this peaceful place alone.

But this burial ground, this final home of some of Talbot County's earliest settlers, is the origin of two of the Easton area's most widely know ghost tales.

Show Me the Way!

The first legend involves a Talbot County country doctor. I've been told this story took place in the 1700s before the days leading up to the Revolution. Another source said the events occurred immediately after the Civil War. And a third tale-teller swore the story occurred during Victorian times.

I have no idea when it happened, but the essence of the tale in all three cases goes something like this.

In the countryside outside of Easton, a certain country doctor was known for more than his medical expertise. Apparently, the gentleman tended to drink too much and it was well known by patients in the region that he often conducted his practice in a less than sober state. However, because he was proficient at his profession—and since there was no other doctor in the area to offer any competition—the locals were tolerant of the old physician's tendency to set a broken bone even if it was obvious that he had recently "tied one on."

Late one evening, a good friend of the doctor was seriously injured while cleaning his gun.

When a nervous stranger awakened the doctor at his office/home and told him of the tragic accident—this was in the days long before telegraph or telephone—the physician was in a seriously loaded state. However, knowing he must do all he could to save his friend, the old doc staggered to his barn, hitched up his faithful horse and headed off in his buggy at top speed. However, since he was pretty well sloshed, the doctor's sense of direction was non-existent. In the darkness of night and his confused state, he became lost. By the time he arrived at his friend's home, the wounded man was dead.

After the death of his friend, the doctor was never the same. According to the legend, to erase the sense of guilt and shame, he drank even more liquor than before the tragedy.

Eventually, late one night, while riding along a narrow back road—probably feeling no pain—the old doctor's horse and carriage wandered off the road and he was killed.

Although the doctor is said to have been buried in the White Marsh church cemetery, many believe that his guilty, intoxicated soul cannot rest. According to the most repeated version of the legend, at various times of the year, area residents and visitors have reported hearing the galloping of an invisible horse.

Still others have said they can hear a ghostly voice shouting, "Show me the way! I'm lost! Quickly! Show me the way!"

Only Asleep

Another ghostly story—told along the Eastern Shore but also repeated often up and down the East Coast from Virginia to Maine—pertains to a woman who died suddenly and was buried in a family plot (or local churchyard, which some in Talbot County believe is the graveyard beside White March Episcopal Church).

As the old story goes, on the evening of her burial, grave robbers opened the freshly dug grave, pried back the coffin lid and began stealing all of the recently departed's valuables. When one robber was unable to separate an expensive ring from the fresh corpse's finger, the robber pulled out his knife and began to cut the jewelry away. While carving off the delicate finger that was swollen under the ring, the robber moved his face close to the stubborn finger.

The sudden pain of the knife blade caused the dead body to rise up and "come back to life." The grave robber standing above the hole was able to escape into the woods—and some say he's still running—but the thieving partner in the hole, who had been carving on the dead woman's ring finger, wasn't as lucky. Terrified that he had awakened the dead, the man stumbled back in fright. Frantic and shouting, he tried in vain to escape from the "vampire woman" and exit from the freshly dug grave. In the confusion, he hit his head on the handle of the shovel while trying to escape from the awakened corpse, and the man fell into the slightly used, but still warm, coffin. Ignoring her bloody, dangling finger, the "dead woman" crawled over the robber's body, climbed out of the fresh grave and headed for home.

When she was found on the front porch, the family took her inside, mended her bloody hand and delighted in her resurrection from the dead.

When the local doctor—not the physician mentioned in the story above—arrived the next day, he announced that the woman had never been dead. Instead, she was a victim of a "coma," a new type of disease. After her sewn finger mended and she caught up on lost sleep, the woman resumed her role as wife and mother.

Meanwhile, the husband and doctor visited the family cemetery to check out the woman's plot. There they found the unconscious body of the grave robber lying in the woman's coffin.

When the husband tried to awaken the man, he discovered a lifeless body. The grave robber was dead—killed by his own knife that was sticking out of his back. Apparently, he had fallen on his weapon in the confusion of trying to escape from the vampire-like woman the night before.

The legend states that the woman, who had been brought back from the dead, lived to a ripe old age and delighted county residents as she repeated her personal experience over and over.

Author's note: In the Talbot County version of this well-know folk story, local and regional newspapers have reported—often during Halloween season that a very similar experience actually occurred to a prominent family who lived in the area several hundred years ago—in the early 1700s. Some residents also believe that the persons who were involved in this mysterious grave robbing incident are buried in the White Marsh Episcopal Church graveyard, off heavily traveled Route 50.

Dog's Best Friend

In the summer of 1964, when Janet was 14 years old, her family took an extended weekend vacation to the mountains of Western Maryland, not far from Grantsville. Since they lived in the city of Baltimore, a weekend in the country was going to be a wonderful adventure. They made arrangements to stay at a four-room cabin owned by a friend of Janet's father.

"When we pulled into the parking area near the front door," Janet recalled, "we were really excited. My sister, Jane, and I started running around the outside of the cabin. But our father's friend, who had met us there, told us to be careful of the tombstones scattered all around the place. He said he didn't want us to trip and fall and get hurt. That got our attention and we settled down immediately."

Janet said the man told them the grave markers indicated the names of dogs that had died and were buried at the site by a previous owner of the cabin.

"At first, the fact that the markers didn't belong to dead people made them seem a little less threatening," Janet said, thinking back several decades. "The man explained that the former owner had loved his dogs, and he wanted to make sure that each of them had a special place to rest when it died."

Janet said that even though there was an innocent explanation for the graves, later in the day she and her sister decided that they still didn't like the idea that they would be sleeping in the middle of a pet cemetery.

"I remember that from the moment we stepped into the cabin," Janet said, "we had a feeling that something was out of sorts. There was a definite chill in the air. And Sammy, our small white dog who came along on the trip, was upset and not acting like his usual happy self."

Janet said that the whole weekend little Sammy seemed to be looking off in the corner of the main room, as if he could see something that no human being could ever be able to visualize. The dog also acted like it could hear things beyond the range of human senses.

"At times," Janet said, "Sammy began to bark continuously, and he acted as if he wanted to go outside to get out of the building. Of course, neither me nor Jane wanted to take him for a walk through the pet graveyard. And Sammy was normally a quiet dog, so all this was very unusual behavior."

The family had planned to stay overnight Friday, Saturday and Sunday and return to Baltimore on Monday morning. On Sunday night, after Janet, Jane and their parents arrived back at the cabin from an early evening dinner, it was dark and spooky.

Sammy had been left in the cabin alone. When the car pulled up in front of the building, there were no sounds at all. It was as if Sammy, who normally became extremely excited and barked loudly when any car came near their home, was not even there.

Worried, the two girls ran up onto the porch and looked into the window.

"We saw Sammy," Janet said, " sitting calmly near the bottom of an overstuffed chair at the feet of an elderly man who was stroking the head of our dog. We turned, shouting to our parents to look inside at the strange man. But by the time they got to the window, the stranger was gone."

Racing into the cabin, the family saw Sammy the dog resting peacefully near the chair. He didn't even get up to acknowledge that the family had come back into the building.

"Sammy had the same contented look on his face that we saw through the window," Janet said. "But there was no stranger anywhere. We looked through all four rooms, but found no one inside. All the doors and windows were locked, just like we had left them. There was no intruder anywhere."

81

The family's last evening in the cabin was a restless one, Janet said. Her father slept in a chair in the living room with Sammy by his side, in case the intruder returned. When they awoke the next morning, no one had any logical explanation for the strange man that the two sisters claimed to have seen.

"As we left that vacation spot," Janet said, "my sister and I were sure of what we had seen the night before. To this very day, I swear that there was a kind, gentle older man stroking Sammy's back. I remember that the man had a smile on his face. Maybe our dog reminded him of one of his dogs. Maybe Sammy was upset that we were gone having dinner and left him behind. The poor animal was all alone in a strange place.

"Perhaps the soul or spirit of the old man who had owned the cabin—and who had loved his dogs so much—came back, even if just for a short time, from beyond the grave to care for Sammy on that one particular night."

No one will ever know for sure.

But no one will ever convince Janet that she didn't see the ghost of the best friend of the dogs whose names are carved in handmade tombstones scattered beside a lonely cabin in the woods north of Grantsville.

The Blue Man

I t was the final morning of Gettysburg Ghost Conference 2000, on a Sunday in the middle of March. I was in the lower level hallway of the Holiday Inn, attempting to leave. A young woman, who introduced herself as Stephanie, stopped me and placed a sealed envelope into my hand.

"Here," she said. "This is my story. Read it. If you want to talk to me, my number's inside."

Obviously, the thin, red-haired woman of about 35 didn't want to talk to me at that time, for she turned and disappeared into the ladies room. Interested in hitting the road after a long weekend in the historic town, I decided not to wait for Stephanie to reappear, shoved her mystery envelope in my jacket pocket, walked to the parking lot, got into my car and pointed it towards Delmarva.

When I returned home, there was the confusion associated with unpacking, sorting out notes and messages and adding new names to my mailing list. Initially, I had forgotten about Stephanie's sealed message, but by Wednesday night, when life was back to normal, I opened her letter and began to read the mystery lady's message, which was fascinating.

It stated:

"I am in my mid 30s now, but I feel I have been through so much in my life that I am much older spirit-wise. My experiences cover a wide range—

83

from hearing voices, seeing apparitions, feeling spirits, pet telepathy, closet portals, psychic dreams and
attacks, not to mention the everyday ESP-type incidents.

"I am unsure of which stories you would like to
hear, but I have two in particular that I think might
interest you. The first one deals with several haunted
dolls and the Blue Man that came along with them.
The second story starts when I was 13, and involves
a spirit who entered my life through an Ouija board
session. This is a long story, and to this day I don't
like mentioning the name of the spirit that was
attached to me for several years. But I will tell you
about him if you are interested in hearing the entire
story."

Within a half hour, I had called Stephanie at her home and
arranged to meet her that weekend, when we would talk about her
experiences in more detail.

The exterior of Stephanie's modern townhouse just outside
the city limits of Annapolis bore no resemblance to the decor of
the building's interior. As I entered the narrow hallway, I was
amazed at the decor that gave this modern, 20th-century building
an authentic Victorian appearance.

Red and gold wallpaper was accented by dark wood trim.
Ornate lamps and heavy curtains with gold fringe reminded me of
sitting rooms of several haunted inns where I had stayed.

After a quick tour of her home, the dental hygienist directed
me to a large, round antique table where I took notes as my hostess described a series of experiences that began when she was
about 10 years old.

"I think I'll tell you about the Blue Man first," she said, indicating that it was one of her more recent experiences. Although it
wasn't the "most significant or threatening," she said, "it can give
us a frame of reference."

I had no objection and listened as Stephanie explained that
she was introduced to my books through the original volume of
Possessed Possessions. She said that the Blue Man reminded her of a
story from that book. She also said she believed the apparition's
presence caused her to contact me in Gettysburg.

"I live here with my husband and two daughters," she said. "About eight months ago, my next door neighbor, Marge, who was very close to me even though she is older, was moving out of the area. Her husband Richie, had died, and Marge decided to move into a place that was smaller and easy for a widow to maintain. She was getting rid of a lot of her possessions. One day, she came to my door with a box of dolls and said I could have them for the girls. Otherwise, she was going to just throw them out."

Not wanting to seem ungrateful, Stephanie accepted the carton and placed it on the floor in her kitchen. Immediately, she noticed that there were four dolls in the box. Three were somewhat modern, but the fourth was quite a bit older and was more finely made. Stephanie said it looked like a Madame Alexander doll, the type that collectors seemed to be interested in at antique shows.

"However, they also were pretty dirty," she recalled. "I didn't want the girls playing with them until I cleaned them up. Who knows where they had been or what could have been crawling over them? I removed the dolls from the box, dusted them off quickly and decided to place them in my bedroom closet—until I had a chance to wash them up properly. But," Stephanie paused, "I remember one strange thing. When I was placing them in the bottom of my closet, I had the feeling that their eyes were staring right through me. The eyes, especially the ones on that older doll, were quite piercing—penetrating to the degree that I found it a bit bothersome. So I placed a towel over the dolls' heads when I put them in the closet."

Prefacing the next statement with, "Now you're going to think I'm crazy," she spoke about the annoying feeling she began to feel each time she entered her bedroom after the dolls arrived. Eventually, she started to avoid opening the closet and she decided that her uneasiness was because of the presence of the dolls.

"Every time I had to go into that room," she said, "I could feel the tension in the air. After four days of this heavy, overpowering ill feeling, I woke up in the middle of the night and there was a large man standing at the foot of my bed."

Stephanie said that even though her husband, Dennis, was lying beside her, she was unable to move or speak. She couldn't alert her husband, so Dennis never saw the phantom visitor.

"When the man—I call him the Blue Man because he had a bluish glow to him, was there—I could not function. In fact, the room was deathly quiet, like a graveyard. We have a fan that runs in the room all the time, for background noise, and it was so quiet in the house that I couldn't even hear the fan noise. But the man was large and glowing. I could only see his head and chest. It was like he didn't have any legs. But it looked just like Marge's dead husband Richie. I could see the thing's eyes, and I swear they were looking directly at me."

Stephanie said she closed her own eyes for a few seconds, reopened them, and the apparition was still there. She said she did this three times, and the ghost of Richie remained in place.

"That's unusual," she said, "because most people say a ghostly figure doesn't stay around that long, especially once it's been noticed. But this one was just standing there, glowing. I got the impression that he wanted me to know he was there."

Getting very little sleep for the rest of the night, and getting no help from her husband who was in La La Land, Stephanie said she spent the rest of what should have been her resting time trying to figure out how and why the spirit had come into her home.

"The only thing that I decided was different," she said, "was the presence of the dolls. Ever since I took them in, things weren't right. And since the spirit visitor looked just like Marge's dead husband, I decided that he had come back looking for his possessions. Maybe he was the one who collected them. I don't know. All I know is that I couldn't think of any other answer. Luckily since the next day was trash day, I put all of them in a big plastic bag and tossed them out."

When I asked her how she could be sure it was the dolls, Stephanie said she didn't have to be certain.

"I have two small girls," she said. "I wasn't taking any chances, and I wasn't going to take my time about sorting things out and considering a number of possibilities. Besides, the dolls gave me the creeps right away. So out they went. As far as I'm concerned, I made the right decision, or I made a lucky guess, because there were no more bad dreams, no more tension in the room and no more visits from the Blue Man."

I asked Stephanie if she ever speculates about what happened to the bothersome dolls. Perhaps they ended up being someone else's problem.

"I wonder about that sometime," she said. "For a few days I thought what may have happened if the trash man discovered them and took them home to his children. But I told myself that maybe he wasn't as receptive to the other side as I am, and he probably didn't have any trouble. Since you asked me, and to be honest about it, I have to admit that I wonder about the dolls and what happened to them a lot. I also wonder why Richie's ghost wanted me to see him. I'll probably never know the answer, just like I can't figure out a lot of things that have happened to me."

Author's note: The story of Stephanie's experiences following her session on a Ouija board will be featured in *Seance in the Study*, Vol. X of the *Spirits Between the Bays* series.

Short Sightings

The 'Unquiet Grave'
St. Augustine, Maryland

Most people have never heard of St. Augustine, Maryland. If you need to find it, check out the official state road map. The hamlet isn't listed in the larger publications like the *Rand McNally Atlas* or the AAA Mid-Atlantic vacation guide. Those publications concentrate on major and medium-sized cities offering popular attractions and scenic daytrips.

St. Augustine is the kind of place you have to go out of your way to find. It is a real place, and part of the village is still there, right in the middle of Cecil County horse country and away from heavy traffic. It's worth visiting any time of year, and as is the case with most pre-Colonial era sites, it may be small but it can offer a wealth of history.

One wonderful thing about studying the past, if you find something recorded you can visit the exact location where history happened. Keep in mind there's a very good chance it will look totally different than it did when the historian recorded his original observations. Just as time doesn't stop, neither does progress—the great destroyer of folklore and our important historic past.

In place of a hand-crafted covered bridge we get a prefabricated interstate highway exit ramp. Over top of a family farm grave plot we end up with a dull bi-level in the midst of a suburban development. Covering a centuries-old earthen fortification on the river's edge we find a high-rise condominium or an office building with a spectacular view of a shopping center-style harbor.

All of these are tradeoffs that people in decision making positions have decided are best for us. So much for progress.

Despite the modern world's efforts to pave the planet, the original historic place hasn't moved. And armed with yellowed documents, old maps, newspaper clippings, black-and-white photographs and a healthy imagination, you can sometimes stand at the very same site and get a sense of what was there long before anyone alive today took a breath.

Such is the case with St. Augustine.

The sleepy crossroads still hosts a few homes and the remnants of the old church.

While the original Manor Chapel of worship is gone, visitors can walk the land near a small white wooden church and read the worn inscriptions of common folks and local heroes who are buried beneath the Eastern Shore soil.

According to *The Manor Chapel or St. Augustine Church*, which was written in 1932 by Effie De Coursey Le Fevre, many historical figures are buried in the graveyard at this quiet country crossroads. Col. Edward Oldham, a descendant of Augustus Herman and a soldier in the Continental Army, rests here. So is Capt. John Thomspon Wirt, veteran of the War of 1812. Among the other officers is Capt. Lucian M. Bean, of the Army of the Confederate States of America, and Union Civil War veterans James A. Warner, Thomas W. Murray and Samuel Simmons.

But it is the "Unquiet Grave" that visitors should seek during their St. Augustine visitation. For its legend has been told and retold for the last 150 years, and it is worth repeating.

As the story goes, a young man who lived a few miles from the village was stricken by a strange disease. He had lived a wild, carefree and wicked life, and his family had prepared him for the death that was approaching with certainty and speed.

According to legend, the frightened young man asked that after his church burial service, when his body was placed in the ground, that no nails or screws be used to seal his coffin lid. He also demanded that no dirt be dropped upon the top of his coffin, and that he be buried in a shallow grave with a small, elevated, rectangular brick wall built around his gravesite. He further stated that the small brick wall extend several layers above the church graveyard ground.

Of course, a flat slab of granite was to be placed over the young man's grave, but he requested that one brick be left out of the wall surrounding his gravesite.

In that way, he said, when the devil came into the tomb to take away his soul, he would be able to escape the clutches of Satan through the opening created by the missing brick.

Even today, after nearly a century and a half, some visitors who come to St. Augustine Churchyard to perform tombstone rubbings, to look at the historic site and to locate the final resting place of their ancestors, have walked away wondering why there is a single brick missing from the tomb that locals still call the "Unquiet Grave."

Diabolical Double

Southern New Hampshire

In the countryside of southern New Hampshire, a college professor decided to build an exact replica of a home in which he had lived in Virginia.

The gentleman had saved the plans, so when he moved into the New England area he assumed it would not take very long to get construction started on his new, duplicate home.

As soon as the well was drilled, the contractor connected it to the hot water heater and other pipes feeding the home. Within two days, dark red water emptied out of every faucet in the house and soon afterwards the well collapsed.

Within the next single week, a series of other unusual mishaps occurred to craftsmen working on the job.

• A carpenter fell down a set of stairs and was bruised and hurt.

• While opening a crank-out window, a painter noticed that the entire unit was falling away from the house. Instinctively, he tried to grab the unit to keep it from falling. As a result, the painter fell out the window opening onto a trash pile beside the house on the ground below.

• A stone mason, who had never missed work, was out sick for four days with a strange and sudden illness.

• The other mason, who as a result of his partner's absence had to complete the decorative interior fireplace work alone, placed a large stone on a high ledge. Later in the day, it fell and landed on the worker's foot, causing it to swell and making the worker limp around on the injured limb.

• A plumber working on the gas line into the fireplace, for some unknown reason, grabbed the rough exposed thread of a pipe and he lacerated his hand. He had to visit a nearby hospital and receive several stitches.

• One worker, who was driving his new pickup truck on the job site, was inside the cab when the accelerator pedal suddenly slammed down against the floor and the truck took off.

• When the workcrew poured the floor for the three-car garage, they estimated short on the amount of concrete that was needed. When they called for an additional truckload, the first vehicle broke down and the second one arrived too late, causing major repairs associated with the garage floor.

Ralph, one of the masons on the job, said, "This was very unusual, because all the people working on this job were experienced. There were no apprentices. These guys were professionals, knew what they were doing. They don't make stupid mistakes. Windows don't fall out because someone forgot to nail them in place. Carpenters don't fall off of stairs or ledges; painters don't fall out of windows. We rarely estimate short when we're pouring a floor. Sure, things happen, but not all at one time, like this.

"Everybody thought it was kind of weird. It was like the whole project, the whole job, was cursed from the beginning. Some people said it was because the house might have been built over some sacred Indian land. It's as good an explanation as any, I guess. And all this happened during the week I was there, building the fireplace. I wonder what other crazy stuff happened over the whole course of the job."

Perhaps the most bizarre part of Ralph's story has nothing to do with the home's construction, but with what happened after the house was completed. "I heard that the guy moved in and sold it very shortly after that," Ralph said. "That's unusual, to have an exact duplicate made of the house you loved so much and then move out. There's got to be more to this story than the little I know."

What's Under My House?

New Castle County, Delaware

Often, people who have an unusual experience and begin to think their house is inhabited by ghosts believe that they must be living over an old cemetery or graveyard.

This isn't always the case. There are other causes of bizarre events. Here is one example.

One evening I received a call from a young woman who lives in a relatively new development home off Route 13, in southern New Castle County, Delaware. When I asked her how she got my name, she explained that she had called her local library and began asking how she could find out about the land where her house was built.

When the reference librarian pressed the woman for a more specific reason for her interest in the area's history, the young woman finally admitted, "I think I have a ghost, and I want to find out if I'm living over a cemetery."

By the time I got the call, the young woman—let's call her Jodie—was quite upset and frustrated. She explained that she was a young mother, who had just moved into the area with her family from Georgia.

"I was standing out on my back patio," Jodie said, "smoking a cigarette, when I turned and saw a little boy. He was dressed in old-fashioned farm clothes, and he was only a few feet away, looking at me from inside my own house."

Shocked and frightened, Jodie tossed down her smoke and raced into the house looking around for the little farm boy, but there was no one else in the home. Her children were in school and her husband was at work. She was there alone.

"That was the only time I witnessed a complete sighting," Jodie said, her voice still a bit nervous. "I just want to find out what's under this place. Maybe we've been built over the little boy's grave and he's upset and that's why he's going to haunt us."

Since that first and only sighting, Jodie said she has seen small glimpses of something moving, out of the corner of her eye. But when she has turned to check it out, there's nothing there.

"I don't know what to do."

I explained that I had not received any other reports of unusual incidents in her development. I also said I did not know of any battles or historic activity on her land. Sometimes an old forgotten pauper's field, a Revolutionary War field hospital or even an old pet cemetery can be part, or all, of the cause of a contemporary home's eerie incidents.

Then, just before she hung up, she asked, "One other thing. Do you think I could have brought the ghost with me?"

When I asked Jodie why she would toss out such a question, she explained that they had lived in an old Georgia farmhouse that everyone said was haunted. All of the neighbors and Jodie's relatives had advised her to move away because the structure had been bad luck for a number of families who had lived there in the past.

"My little boy told me that he had an invisible playmate," she said. "We used to laugh at him until he ran into our bedroom and told us that his bed was floating into the air and moving across the room," Jodie said. "Once, he came rushing in and said that he had to jump off of his bed before it hit the ceiling. About a minute later we heard a big thump, like furniture hitting the floor."

Considering those comments, I told Jodie to observe her son carefully and to ask him if his "little friend" from Georgia had made the trip north to Delaware. That might be the answer to her problems—but it's certainly not the solution.

Where are the Rings?

Lancaster County, Pa.

Will currently lives in Delaware, but he used to make his home in Lititz, Pa., a small town directly north of Lancaster. At the very beginning of our conversation, Will said he wanted me to know that he has an open mind. That means he's not a confirmed believer in ghosts, but he admits there's a good possibility that sometimes strange, or unexplainable events, can happen. In fact, he said he's been bothered for more than 15 years by the bizarre incident that occurred to him one evening in his in-law's Lancaster County Victorian-era home.

Will's father-in-law, Mike, had just died and Will and his wife, Cheryl, were staying at his mother-in-law's home the night before the funeral. The widow, who's name was Sarah, didn't want to be alone. Will and Cheryl decided it would best if they kept the older woman company during the difficult time.

"I remember sitting at the kitchen table, in the back of the house, and seeing Sarah wringing her hands and explaining that she was very worried since she couldn't find her husband's rings," Will said. "Sarah told us it was very important that she get them to the undertaker first thing the following morning, so he could put them on Mike before they closed the coffin and left for the church.

"I didn't think there was anything I could do," Will recalled, "so I just sat there while my wife and her mother methodically went through every room on the first and second floors looking for Mike's rings."

After about 45 minutes, the two women returned empty handed. They had no luck in locating the jewelry. Frustrated but determined, they decided to have a second look. Again they returned to the kitchen without the rings.

"After the second search," Will said, "I remember looking at Sarah, who was wringing her hands in worry, standing beside the kitchen sink. I suddenly stood up, walked into the dining room and reached into a small square drawer of an old treadle sewing machine. Calmly, I retrieved the two rings, returned to the kitchen and placed them into Sarah's hands."

Astonished, Sarah asked Will how he knew where to look. But he replied he didn't know why he had gotten up or how he had found them.

"I can honestly say," Will said, "that I had no thought at all in my mind when I acted. In fact, it was probably the only time in my life that my mind was completely blank. I really had no idea of what I had done until I gave Sarah the two rings."

Squeezing the precious rings in her hand, Sarah said she remembered placing the rings in the old sewing machine drawer for safe keeping. It had happened when Mike had come home from the hospital and they had set a hospital bed up for him in the dining room. As soon as Mike arrived, to make him more comfortable, Sarah took the rings off her husband's swollen fingers.

Will admitted he has searched for a reason behind his ability to locate the rings.

He had no idea that Mike was using the dining room as a sick room. He also had never looked inside the sewing machine until the day when he located the missing rings.

"I've turned this over in my mind for years," Will said. "There is no way I could have known where the rings were. But two things stand out in my mind. Mike and I got along very well. We were as comfortable as any in-laws could be, and we would spend hours together watching sports and talking while the women were out shopping or spending time together. He was a kind, good man— well respected, decent. We enjoyed being together.

"The other thing is, Mike made taking care of Sarah his main priority. He never wanted her to worry about anything. If she wanted something done around the house, he would do it and do it quickly. He went to almost any lengths to correct anything that might worry her."

Pausing, Will looked across the table at me and said, "A part of me truly believes that Mike, or his spirit, could tell somehow that Sarah was disturbed. And his final act was to use me to do something about it. I'm not sure, of course, but I don't have a better answer."

More Incidents at Fort Delaware

Pea Patch Island, Delaware

Each year, more unusual stories are added to the lore of Fort Delaware, the former Civil War-era island prison camp that held more than 33,000 captured Confederate soldiers.

Since 1997, I have been co-host, along with Fort Delaware State Park historian and author Dale Fetzer, of the popular Friday evening Ghost Lantern Tours that take place on Pea Patch Island, in the middle of the Delaware River.

Visitors have had sightings of Rebel and Union soldiers and the infamous "Man in the Black Cloak." Tourists have mailed us photographs featuring energy-filled orbs, shadowy figures, leaping flames from the kitchen fireplace and even the apparition of a soldier standing beside a cannon on the fort's parade ground.

All of these stories have been detailed in Volumes III, VI, VII and VIII of this *Spirits Between the Bays* ghost/folklore series.

Since our last book, *Horror in the Hallway*, two new incidents have occurred and are worth sharing.

The first involves Dale Fetzer, who gives a presentation of Edgar Allan Poe on the Saturday nights of the special Halloween programs.

On Halloween night, while Dale was presenting his Poe program, all the lights went out, but he continued with the presentation using candlelight, which was quiet effective. Later, two couples were talking to him, discussing the show and how much they had enjoyed it.

One of the gentlemen said he especially liked how the woman in old-fashioned clothing came out and dusted off the mantle. She looked very authentic, the man said.

Surprised, Dale informed the man that there was no woman dusting off the mantle. To his further surprise, the other people who had accompanied the first gentleman to the show said they, too, had seen the mysterious woman dusting the mantle the evening of Dales' performance.

But she was not in the script.

The second event involved a young man who took the summer tour with his wife and returned to the island during late October to see the Halloween program.

At the end of the evening, as we sat together on a bench in the lower deck of the *Delafort*, the ferry that transports visitors to and from the island, the young man asked if I had ever come up with an explanation to his summer sighting.

The incident had occurred while Dale was presenting his General Albin Schoepf interpretation in the restored Fort Delaware Commandant's Office. Dale's program takes place in the midpoint of the tour, and he is surrounded by about 90 people who crowd into two large rooms filled with antique furniture, uniforms and photographs.

During Dale's speech, the young man said he saw something move beneath one of the tables. When he looked down, the man saw a pale white face of a ghostly figure. Then, when he looked back under the table to get a better view, whatever it was had disappeared. The man swore, during both our summer and late October conversations, that he was positive of his observation. The sighting was not the product of an overactive imagination and he had been bothered by the sight ever since.

I tried to assure him there was no one assigned to play the part of a ghost under any of the Fort Delaware furniture. And even if there were, how could such a creature disappear in the midst of a room filled with people?

About the Author

Ed Okonowicz, a Delaware native,is an editor and writer at the University of Delaware, where he also teaches story-telling and feature writing classes.

A professional storyteller, Ed presents programs at country inns and retirement homes, in schools, libraries and theaters and for private events, Elderhostels. conventions and dinner meetings in the Mid-Atlantic region.

He specializes in local legends and folklore of the Delmarva Peninsula. His original story, "Concert by Candlelight," which is featured in Vol. III, *Welcome Inn*, won an Honor Award from *Storytelling World Magazine*.

Ed also conducts special training courses and workshops for historical societies and museums, where he shows how story-telling techniques can be used by tour guides and instructors. Since 1997. he has helped develop and conduct fund raising ghost tours with historians at Fort Delaware and town and cemetery tours in Elkton, Maryland.

About the Artist

Kathleen Burgoon Okonowicz, a watercolor artist and illustrator, is originally from Greenbelt, Maryland. She studied art in high school and college, and is an artist member of the Baltimore Watercolor Society. Her style focuses on realism and detail.

Kathleen enjoys taking things of the past and preserving them in her paintings. Her philosophy is evident in both of her full-color limited edition prints. Her print, *Special Places*, features the stately stairway in Wilmington, Delaware, that was the "special place" of the characters in Ed's love story, *Stairway over the Brandywine*. Last fall she released *Station No. 5*, a print that captures the charm of a 1893 Victorian-style firehouse also in Wilmington, near Trolley Square.

A graduate of Salisbury State University, Kathleen earned her master's degree in professional writing from Towson State University. In addition to painting, she teaches a self-publishing course at the University of Delaware.,

---

For information on storytelling, call Ed. For self-publishing or graphic design assistance, call Kathleen.
Telephone: 410 398-5013.

True Ghost Stories from Master Storyteller
Ed Okonowicz

Chills await you in each volume.

Wander through the rooms, hallways and dark corners of this eerie series.

Creep deeper and deeper into terror, until you run *Down the Stairs and Out the Door* in the last volume of our 13-book series of ghostly tales of the Mid-Atlantic region.

Storytelling World
Honor Award

Delaware Press Association
First Place Award
1997

Delaware Press Association
First Place Award
1998

$\mathcal{S}$*pirits*
Between the Bays
Series

Volume by volume our haunted house grows. Enter at your own risk!

"If this collection doesn't give you a chill, check your pulse, you might be dead."
—Leslie R. McNair
The Review, University of Delaware

"This expert storyteller can even make a vanishing hitchhiker story fresh and startling."
—Chris Woodyard
owner of Invisible Ink Ghost Catalog
and author of *Haunted Ohio* series

COMING NEXT: SEANCE IN THE STUDY

Delaware Press Association
Second Place Award
2000

Delaware Press Association
First Place Award
2000

The Original

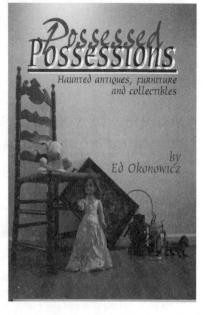

Possessed Possessions

Haunted antiques, furniture and collectibles

by
Ed Okonowicz

A BUMP. A THUD. MYSTERIOUS MOVEMENT. Unexplained happenings. Caused by What? Venture through this collection of short stories and discover the answer. Experience 20 eerie, true tales about items from across the country that, apparently, have taken on an independent spirit of their own—for they refuse to give up the ghost.

From Maine to Florida, from Pennsylvania to Wisconsin . . haunted heirlooms exist among us . . . everywhere.

Read about them in *Possessed Possessions*, the book some antique dealers *definitely* do not want you to buy.

$9.95

112 pages
5 1/2" x 8 1/2"
softcover
ISBN 0-9643244-5-8

Now the Sequel

ISBN 0-890690-02-3

A<small>CROSS THE</small> <small>ENTIRE</small> <small>COUNTRY,</small>
<small>POSSESSED</small> <small>POSSESSIONS</small>
<small>CONTINUE TO</small> <small>APPEAR.</small>

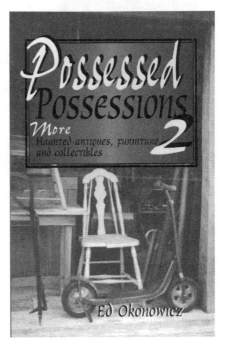

Read about 40 more amazing
true tales of bizarre, unusual
and unexplained incidents—all
caused by haunted objects like:
demented dolls
spirited sculptures
pesky piano
killer crib
and much, much more

112 pages
5 1/2" x 8 1/2"
softcover
ISBN 0-890690-02-3

$9.95

WARNING

There could be more than just dust hovering around some of
the items in your home.

The DelMarVa Murder Mystery series

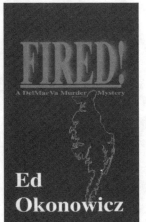

Ed Okonowicz

1998

320 pages
4 1/4" x 6 3/4"
softcover
ISBN 1-890690-01-5

$9.95

Early in the 21st century, DelMarVa, the newest state in the union, which includes Delaware and the Eastern Shore of Maryland and Virginia, is plagued by a ruthless serial killer. In FIRED! meet Gov. Henry McDevitt, Police Commissioner Michael Pentak and State Psychologist Stephanie Litera as they track down the peninsula's worst killer since 19th century murderess Patty Cannon.

In *Halloween House*, the series continues as Gov. McDevitt, Commissioner Pentak and other DelMarVa crime fighters go up against Craig Dire, a demented businessman who turns his annual Halloween show into a real-life chamber of horrors.

Delaware Press Association First Place Award 2000

1999

320 pages
4 1/4" x 6 3/4"
softcover
ISBN 1-890690-03-1

$9.95

The DelMarVa Murder Mystery series continues in the Spring of 2001 with **HOSTAGE,** set at Fort Delaware on Pea Patch Island.

WELCOME

to the

State of

DelMarVa

FIRED!

". . . this is Okonowicz's
best book so far!"
—The Star Democrat
Easton, Md.

"Lots of familiar places
in this imaginative
suspense novel."
—Jeannine Lahey
About.com
Wilmington, Del.

"Politics and romance make
fairly strange bedfellows, but
add a dash of mystery and
mahem and the result can be
spectacular, as evidenced in
FIRED!"
—Sharon Galligar Chance
BookBrowser Review

Halloween House

"Halloween House *mystery*
Chills summer heat."
—Rosanne Pack
Cape Gazette

"Looking at the front cover, the
reader knows it's going to be a
bumpy night."
—Erika Quesenbery
The Herald

MURDER, MYSTERY, MUTILATIONS AND MORE . . . IN YOUR OWN BACKYARD

103

Disappearing Delmarva
Portraits of the Peninsula People

Photography and stories by
Ed Okonowicz

Disappearing Delmarva introduces you to more than 70 people on the peninsula whose professions are endangered. Their work, words and wisdom are captured in the 208 pages of this hardbound volume, which features more than 60 photographs.

Along the back roads and back creeks of Delaware, Maryland, and Virginia—in such hamlets as Felton and Blackbird in Delaware, Taylors Island and North East in Maryland, and Chincoteague and Sanford in Virginia—these colorful residents still work at the trades that have been passed down to them by grandparents and elders.

208 pages
8 1/2" x 11"
Hardcover
ISBN 1-890690-00-7

$38.00

Ed presents a program based on this award-winning book at local historical societies and libraries. Contact him at 410 398-5013 to arrange a program in your area.

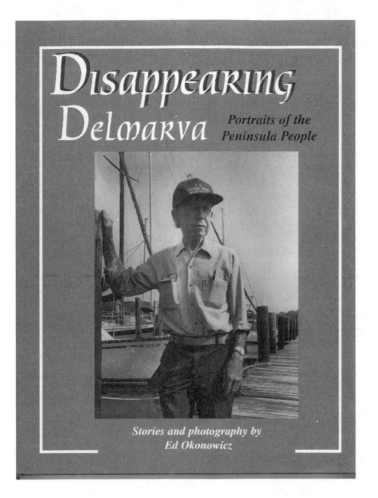

Stories and photography by
Ed Okonowicz

Winner of 2 First-Place Awards:

Best *general book*
Best *Photojournalism entry*

National Federation of Press Women Inc.
1998 Communication Contest

To complete your collection. . .
or to tell us about *your* ghostly experience, use the form below:

Name _____

Address_____

City_____State_____Zip Code_____

Phone Numbers _(_____)_____(_____)_____
          Day   Evening

_____I would like to be placed on the mailing list to receive the free
          Spirits Speaks newsletter and information on future volumes.

_____I have an experience I would like to share. Please call me.
          (Each person who sends in a submission will be contacted. If your
          story is used, you will receive a free copy of the volume in which your
          experience appears.)

I would like to order the following books:

Quantity	Title	Price	Total
_____	Pulling Back the Curtain, Vol I	$ 8.95	_____
_____	Opening the Door, Vol II	$ 8.95	_____
_____	Welcome Inn, Vol III	$ 8.95	_____
_____	In the Vestibule, Vol IV	$ 9.95	_____
_____	Presence in the Parlor, Vol V	$ 9.95	_____
_____	Crying in the Kitchen, Vol VI	$ 9.95	_____
_____	Up the Back Stairway, Vol VII	$ 9.95	_____
_____	Horror in the Hallway, Vol VIII	$ 9.95	_____
_____	**Phantom in the Bedchamber, Vol IX**	**$ 9.95**	_____
_____	Possessed Possessions	$ 9.95	_____
_____	Possessed Possessions 2	$ 9.95	_____
_____	Fired! A DelMarVa Murder Mystery(DMM)	$ 9.95	_____
_____	Halloween House DMM#2	$ 9.95	_____
_____	Disappearing Delmarva	$38.00	_____
_____	Stairway over the Brandywine, A Love Story	$ 5.00	_____

*Md residents add 5% sales tax.
Please include $1.50 postage for the first book,
and 50 cents for each additional book.
Make checks payable to:
Myst and Lace Publishers

Subtotal_____
Tax*_____
Shipping_____
Total_____

All books are signed by the author. If you would like the book(s) personalized,
please specify to whom.

Mail to: Ed Okonowicz
1386 Fair Hill Lane
Elkton, Maryland 21921